Whiskey Tribute

A TRIDENT SECURITY NOVELLA - BOOK 5.5

BY SAMANTHA A. COLE

i

Any information regarding persons or places has been used with creative literary license so there may be discrepancies between fiction and reality. The Navy SEALs missions and personal qualities within have been created to enhance the story and, again, may be exaggerated and not coincide with reality.

The author has full respect for the members of the United States Military and the varied members of law enforcement and thanks them for their continuing service to making this country as safe and free as possible.

DEDICATION

To my readers…thank you for asking for more stories from my characters!

TABLE OF CONTENTS

ACKNOWLEDGEMENTS

As always, I want to thank the following:

My beta readers;

My editor, Eve;

My Facebook group, The Sexy-Six-Pack Sirens;

My family;

My friends;

And most of all, my readers!

CHAPTER 1

Flush against the wall of the shed separating his teammate and him from their sworn enemy, Curt 'Elmer' Bannerman peeked around the corner, searching for a target. There was nobody in sight, but it didn't mean they weren't out there. There were plenty of places to hide, so the tangos could be anywhere. Glancing at his partner, standing stoically beside him, weapon in hand, he cocked his head toward their destination. "We're going to make a run for that boulder over there. Keep low. Ready?"

The response he got was a nod of the head and a muttered "yup."

"Count of three. One. Two. Three. Go!"

Zig-zagging across the expanse, they were almost to safety when he realized he'd run them right into an ambush. *Shit!* He blocked his partner with his bigger body, ready to defend with his life, and was hit dead in the chest by an exploding projectile. Stunned he'd been caught with his proverbial pants down, he grabbed his sternum and fell to his knees.

"I got you!"

Cheers were followed by laughter and giggles as the Prichard kids all came out of hiding and bombarded him with snowballs while celebrating nine-year-old Justin's successful throw, which took down the former Navy SEAL. Even his partner, six-year-old Amanda, had turned traitorous and dropped her snowball on his head.

"Ouch! Come here, you." He playfully reached for the little pixie, but she ran behind her second oldest brother, ten-year-old Taylor, for protection, squealing the whole way. Twelve-year-old Ryan and his brothers continued to pelt Curt with snowballs, so he let Amanda get away, then rolled to his feet and quickly returned fire, making sure he didn't hit anyone in the head.

Their mother, Dana, stuck her head out the back door of the old farmhouse, which was no longer part of a farm, aside from a few chickens and one cocky rooster. "Dinner's ready! Come and get it!"

The kids whooped it up in unison. Apparently they'd worked up appetites, which were as big as Curt's own. He knew Dana had made her famous beef stew, and his mouth was watering just knowing it was inside waiting for them. Or maybe it was the chef who was making his mouth water. *Knock it off, asshole. She's your best friend's wife and, therefore, off-limits.*

While the kids ran inside, Curt ambled over to where his old teammate, Marco 'Polo' DeAngelis, was stacking the last of the firewood the two of them had cut up before the kids had come out to play. They'd made the trip up to Stormville, Iowa, yesterday from Florida. Marco from Tampa and Curt from Daytona Beach. As a retired Navy SEALs from Team Four, they were taking care of the family of one of their own—one of the fallen. Eric Prichard, Curt's best friend since basic training, had been murdered by an assassin over a year ago, in what had originally looked like a hit-and-run accident.

Eric had been doing his evening run when he was struck and killed by an unknown vehicle. It was later learned that seven former members of Team Four had been targeted because of a mission they'd been on years ago. Three of the seven had been killed before the rest of them figured things out and the threat was eliminated. Curt didn't know all of the details, as the resulting investigation was deemed classified by the government. But his former lieutenant, and Marco's current boss at Trident Security, Ian Sawyer, had discreetly let him know Eric's death had been avenged—justice had been served.

Immediately following Eric's funeral, a bunch of his former teammates had put together a rotating schedule. Twice a month, two of them would head up here and stay at a local motel. They would then spend the weekend doing everything around the house and property Eric could no longer do for his family. A new roof had been put up, the main bathroom had been renovated, and the landscaping was tended to. If there was nothing pressing that needed to be done, whoever's weekend it was would do something fun with the family, like camping or a trip to Six-Flags. Today, Marco and he had spent the morning making fast work of painting little Amanda's room pink and purple. She'd been making it known for several weeks she was now too big for the Winnie the Pooh theme she'd had for the past four years.

Curt approached his buddy while brushing the snow from his blond hair. "Hand me the axes. I'll put them in the shed. You're looking a little hypothermic there, Polo."

"Ya think?" the man snorted, his Staten Island accent coming through. "It's colder than a witch's tit out here. I knew there was a reason I moved to the Sunshine State."

Chuckling, Curt bent over and pulled one of the axes out of the old tree stump they'd used, then took the one Marco handed him. "I could get used to it again. You forget—I'm from Montana. This is nothing— a tropical heat wave."

"Yeah, well…why don't you stop ogling the merry widow, tell her how you feel, and then you can live in the Tropics of Iowa all year round."

Even though his cheeks were red from the cold, the six-foot-four, two-hundred-twenty-pound man blushed. Was it that fucking obvious he had a hard time keeping his eyes in his sockets when Dana was around? *Shit.* And when the fuck had that started? Yeah, she was attractive…hell, she was hot—always had been. Even though she still carried around some of the weight she'd gained during her four pregnancies, her body still rocked. He loved curvaceous women, and she had an awesome hourglass figure. *Shit.* Not wanting to admit his friend was right about the ogling, he lied. "What are you fucking talking about? I'm not interested in Dana."

Crossing his arms, Marco rolled his eyes. "Please. Don't give me that. You get a goofy, fucking grin on your face every time she walks into the room. Probably a fucking hard-on, too, but I have no desire to confirm that by taking a look at your junk. Every time someone can't make it up here for their weekend, you've been filling in. And don't tell me it's because Eric was your best friend."

"He is…was…damn it." Scowling, Curt turned and strode toward the shed, but Marco followed on his heels. *Damn it.* Why couldn't his buddy just drop it? Curt had no business lusting for his best friend's wife. He was here to do right by Eric's family. Nothing more.

"I know he was." Marco's voice was stern, but also filled with sympathy. "But you know better than I do he'd want you to have a good life without him. Same goes for Dana. I've seen the way she looks at you sometimes. And the kids and you get along great—so what's the problem? It's been almost a year and a half since he was killed. Get off your fucking ass, before someone steps in and snatches her up."

What? Curt saw red and whirled around so fast, Marco almost got hit in his cold cock with an ax. "Who's going to snatch her up? Someone else been eyeing her?"

The bastard had the audacity to smirk. "Thought you weren't interested."

"Don't fuck with me, Polo. Who the fuck else is interested in her?"

Clearly finding amusement in Curt's demeanor, the other man shrugged. "I don't know for sure, but Egghead mentioned the Sheriff seemed to be sniffing around a lot when he was up here two weeks ago." Brody 'Egghead' Evans was Marco's best friend and teammate at Trident Security, as well as a former member of Team Four, and was the biggest computer geek in the world—or close to it.

"Fuck that shit." His gaze went to the rear entrance of the house, and the thought of Dana in another man's arms had his blood boiling. He should have known she was going to have guys chasing after her someday, but not this soon. Years ago, he'd promised Eric that if anything happened to him, he would watch over Dana and make sure she and the kids stayed safe and protected. And it was a promise he intended to keep.

Marco slapped him on the shoulder before taking the axes from him. "So, you gonna man-up and tell her how you feel?"

Curt nodded, his eyes never leaving the backdoor. If it kept the other sharks at bay, he'd do what he had to. "Damn, fucking straight."

"About fucking time."

But the moment he stepped into the country kitchen and saw Dana

5

ladling the stew into bowls for everyone, his courage fled. Eric was still here—in every picture, every expression on his children's faces, and in every beat of Dana's heart. He couldn't do it. He couldn't lust after his best friend's wife. Not now...and not even ten years from now. All he could do was keep everything platonic and be her go-to guy when she needed help with anything. *It sucked being a man who always did the right thing.*

* * *

"Uncle Curtsy, can you read me a bedtime story before you leave?"

He ignored Marco's smug grin at the nickname Amanda had been calling him since she'd first been able to say his name. It was embarrassing sometimes, but when his god-daughter looked up at him with those big brown eyes of hers, he just melted. "Sure, sweetheart. Go brush your teeth like your momma told you, and then pick out a book."

Smiling, she ran to the bathroom. The boys were in their bedrooms playing video games as the two men finished putting the last of Amanda's bedroom furniture back where it belonged. Dana had put the new sheets and comforter on the bed, and planned on putting the new curtains up tomorrow. At the moment, she was doing another load of laundry. It amazed him how many clothes four kids could go through in a matter of days.

"So you chickened out, *huh*?"

He'd been wondering when his friend was going to say something. All through dinner, his guilt had been eating at him. He was an asshole, lusting after another man's wife...and not just any man, but one who'd saved his life on a mission gone FUBAR—fucked up beyond all recognition—in Afghanistan. "Shove it, Polo. She's not ready, and even if she was, I can't get past the fact she belongs to Eric."

Marco sighed heavily. "Belonged, man. Past tense."

Pushing a white, straight-back chair under its matching desk, Curt scowled at the other man. "You know, you're the last person I expected to hear shit from about this. Mister I'm-never-getting-married-and-having kids."

The man's childhood had been shitty and the only family he truly had, besides his brothers-in-arms, had been his sister, Nina, who'd passed away of cancer over a year ago. Marco had taken it really rough, and it was a good thing his teammates had been on his six, watching his back and getting him out of his funk.

"Hey, just because I don't want it for me, doesn't mean I don't want my friends to find someone to love." He glanced out the bedroom door to make sure there were no kids lurking about and lowered his voice a little. "But that's what I like about the lifestyle. I can get my rocks off, have a temporary relationship with an end date, and give a woman the care she needs, and what I need to give. Nothing drastic and then I move on. But that's not you, man. You're missing out on something real here. Just because I'm not walking down the aisle doesn't mean I don't recognize when two people belong together."

Curt knew all about the BDSM lifestyle his buddy was talking about, but it had never been for him...or Eric. While neither of them had a problem with some of their teammates going to clubs like that, and even owning one, they hadn't felt the draw to it the others did. Vanilla sex, with the occasional slap and tickle, was fine with him. He just didn't get into the whole Dominant/submissive thing. "Yeah, well, I get the feeling there's some chick out there that's going to turn your world upside down and slap-shit forward. And I'm going to laugh my ass off when it happens. As for me and Dana...never mind—"

He dropped the rest of the conversation when Amanda came skipping in and hurried to her bookshelf. Picking a book, she handed it to him and jumped into her bed, climbing under the fresh sheets. Marco slapped him on the back as he headed toward the door. "I'll see if Dana needs anything else done before we leave. Night, Amanda."

"Night, Uncle Marco." Hugging her favorite stuffed rabbit, she moved to the inside of the twin bed to give him room and then patted the spot next to her. "Sit here, Uncle Curtsy."

Doing as he was told, his elbow accidentally knocked over the 5x7 frame on her nightstand. After setting it right, he stared at the photo of Eric with his then four-year-old daughter on his shoulders. Curt's gut clenched a little. Damn, he missed the guy. *Don't worry, my friend. I'll take care of them.*

CHAPTER 2

Fourteen Years Ago

"Dude, there she is."

Curt didn't know who or what Eric was talking about because he was too busy checking out the new SEAL bunnies who'd shown up at The Clamshell, a bar near the Little Creek, Virginia naval base. There were two categories of bunnies—chicks who wanted to bang a SEAL for bragging rights, and those who wanted to marry one of the elite men. Curt was only interested in the ones in the former group. One-night-stands, maybe a few-night-stands and then move on. At twenty-five, he had no desire to settle down anytime soon.

His buddy smacked his upper arm. "Dude, whatta think?"

"About what?" He winked at a cute, curvy blonde giving him the eye. When she giggled and blushed, he knew he'd found tonight's conquest. While some of the team had gone to a local BDSM club they frequented when the team was INCONUS, a few others had come here instead. Curt had no problem with his teammates being in the lifestyle,

9

he just didn't get the whole concept of it. Yeah, a pair of handcuffs and blindfold could definitely make an evening fun. If a woman wanted to put the cuffs on him and cover his eyes while she sucked him off before riding him cowgirl style, then who was he to complain? But he didn't care for the Master/submissive thing.

"That chick, Dana, I told you about." Eric stood and waved over the crowd. He raised his voice to be heard over the music blaring from the jukebox and the chatter going on around them. "Hey, Dana! Over here!"

Turning his head to see who his friend was yelling at, Curt spotted an attractive brunette weaving through the bar full of patrons on her way to their table. *"That's* the chick with the flat tire you helped fix this morning? Bow-chick-wow-wow. Damn, bro, why doesn't shit like that happen to me with hotties like that? I get the old grannies."

"Shut up, asshole," Eric warned in a low voice just before the pretty, young woman reached them. Being a gentleman, Curt stood as Eric greeted her. "Hey, Dana. Glad you could make it. This is my buddy, Curt Bannerman…*aaaaaand*, I just realized I didn't get your last name earlier."

She smiled at Eric, before holding her hand out to Curt. "It's Goodman. Dana Goodman. Nice to meet you."

"Same here, darling." Now that she was right in front of him, he saw her eyes were the color of milk chocolate. She stood about five-foot-eight and had curves that would have most heterosexual males drooling over her. Glancing around, he saw a lot of the guys ogling her ass and he was tempted to ask her to turn around, so he could check it out himself. *Down boy. Your buddy saw her first. Bros before hoes.*

Eric pulled out a chair for her. "Here. Have a seat. Can I get you something to drink? Elmer grab the waitress so we can get Dana a drink."

Holy crap. Curt eyed his friend with amusement. He'd never seen the guy this nervous around a woman before. Hell, he had never seen him this nervous in combat for fuck's sake. Flagging their waitress, he ordered the rum and coke which Dana asked for and two more beers. Eric was going to need one to chill out.

"Why Elmer?"

"*Huh*? Oh." He took a quick swig of his beer before explaining it to her. "It's my call sign. Back in basic training, I scored the highest in firearms. Our drill instructor asked me where I learned to shoot and I told him I'd been hunting rabbits since I was a kid. So he dubbed me Elmer, as in Elmer Fudd…huntin' wabbits."

She chuckled…not giggled, but chuckled. He knew then and there she wasn't a SEAL bunny—just an honest to goodness woman, who was interested in the guy who had stopped and changed her tire. She eyed Eric with curiosity. "So what about you? What's your call sign? And yes, I know they're call signs and not nicknames. My cousin is in the Navy and serving on a sub somewhere in the Pacific, and my dad's retired from the Air Force."

Eric rolled his eyes. He was one of the guys who got stuck with a call sign he wasn't thrilled with. Unfortunately, you didn't get to pick it, or have any say in the matter, and if you hated what you ended up with, it was all the more reason for everyone to use it. It was best if you didn't bitch about it, either, because you might end up with one even worse than that. "Since Elmer was my best friend since day one of BT, I ended up being tagged 'Wabbit', which I'll never forgive him for."

Laughing, Curt smacked his buddy on the back. "Sure you will, you wascally wabbit!"

"Hey, Dana."

The trio looked up to see two other women, about Dana's

approximate age of twenty-four, had stopped beside the table. Not bad, Curt thought to himself and hoped they would be joining them. The two dark-haired beauties erased the cute blonde at the bar from his mind. Picking which one to hit on was going to be difficult…but enjoyable.

Both Curt and he stood as Dana introduced them to her friends. "Eric and Curt, this is Vanessa and Rebekah. I asked them to meet us if that's okay?"

Her gaze was on Eric as she spoke. She was obviously as hooked on him as he was on her, but she'd still been a smart girl, bringing her friends along, in case the object of her affection turned into a creep—which Curt knew he wouldn't. Eric may have had his share of women dropping at his feet to suck his dick or whatever, but Curt had never heard the man disrespect a woman in the entire time he'd known him. After seven years, he knew the guy well.

While Curt pulled out the chair next to him for one of the women to sit on, Eric snatched another chair from a table behind him. For the next few hours, they all had a great time…and Eric and Dana began to fall in love.

* * *

Eighteen Months Later

"You sure about this, man?" Curt asked Eric as the two of them checked their reflections in the floor length mirror in the sacristy of the church. "You still have a few minutes to make a run for it."

Eric brushed a piece of lint from his dress whites. "No freaking way, dude. She's the one. She's hot, sweet, rocks my world, and doesn't have a problem being a Navy SEAL's wife. My family loves her and she gets along great with them. And to top it all off, I'm madly in love with her. What more could I ask for?"

Shrugging his shoulder, Curt smirked. "I don't know....maybe a twin?"

"Asshole. Oops, sorry, Father."

Neither one of them had heard the older priest come back in. Shaking his head, Father O'Malley chuckled. "No worries. It's something you get used to as a Navy Chaplin. The bride's father just gave me the thumbs up, so I guess it's a go. Ready?"

Taking one last look in the mirror to make sure his uniform was perfect, Eric squared his shoulders and headed for the door to the altar. "As ready as I'll ever be. Let's do it. *Hoo-yah!*"

Curt followed and took his spot next to his best friend, checking his pocket once again for the two rings he'd been placed in charge of. Two more of their Navy buddies had joined them in the bridal party along with one of Eric's cousins, who had donned a grey suit for the occasion. Most of the SEAL team they'd been serving with over the past two years was in attendance, along with fifty of Dana and Curt's friends and family. It wasn't a huge affair, but that's how the couple had wanted it.

The organ music began to play and the bridesmaids made their entrances at the back of the chapel. An adorable six-year-old flower girl skipped up the aisle making everyone smile and laugh. Then the music changed to the bridal march and the crowd stood to watch the bride float down the aisle on her father's arm. She was stunning—and that was an understatement. Curt bumped shoulders with Eric, who couldn't take his eyes off Dana, and whispered, "You were right, man. She's the one."

"Told you."

There wasn't a dry eye in the house as Dana's father, who had been diagnosed with terminal cancer two months earlier, handed her off to her fiancé and good-naturedly saluted him. Eric returned the gesture to the retired Air Force captain, then escorted his bride the last few steps to the altar where the chaplain blessed the couple. After they were pronounced man and wife, the reception went until almost dawn at a nearby hotel. They'd started off in the ballroom, but when their time there ran out, the party was moved to the bar/lounge and the drinks flowed. Curt lost count of the number of whiskey shots the team had thrown back in toasts to the couple. All in all, it had been an awesome night.

CHAPTER 3

Present

"Something like this?" Curt finished sketching the paint job design, and then rotated the pad a hundred and eighty degrees on the counter, so his potential new customer could see it. "I can make any changes you want."

"No, man, this is fucking awesome! It's exactly what I was looking for. You're a fucking genius."

He snorted at the twenty-something-year-old guy, who had been referred by a friend whose motorcycle Curt had detailed a few months ago. "Yeah, I get that a lot."

Flipping the pad back around, he made a few small corrections, then signed the bottom of the page and wrote 'HALO Customs' underneath it. The motorcycle repair and detail shop was the business his brother and he had opened up in Daytona after he'd retired from SEAL Team Four three years ago. Chris was seven years younger than him and had retired from the Army, after being a mechanic for them for eight years. He then apprenticed with a guy who did custom bike jobs, so when Curt got out, they could start the business they'd talked about for years. Chris did all the engine work and body designs, while Curt did all the custom detailing, using the creative skills he'd inherited from their mother, an art teacher. The business had grown over the years, mostly by word-of-mouth, to the point they had eight other guys working for them now. It had been a great relief to him since he didn't have to worry about taking time off here and there to head up to Iowa for long weekends.

"I'm booked solid for the next five weeks." He slid over the large day-planner with his schedule in it. Between their receptionist, Monica, and him, they kept it up-to-date. "The soonest I can get you in is the third week of May. Is that okay with you?"

"That'd be awesome, dude—as long as it's finished before the start of the summer. I've been dying to get this done ever since I saw what you did on my buddy's bike."

Grabbing an invoice pad, Curt wrote down the details of the job and what it would cost. "Here's the estimate. It's subject to any changes you make to the design or add-ons."

The guy looked it over and didn't even flinch at the bottom line. Not that Curt expected him to, with what the motorcycle had cost in the first place. The Seventy-Two Harley, with all the bells and whistles, had to have set him back, at least $25,000 when he bought it a few months ago, and that was including the custom paint job he was now replacing.

Sitting on the side shelf of his draft table, his cell phone rang, and he glanced at the screen. *Devon Sawyer*. He picked up the device and hit the button to connect the call. "Hey, Devil Dog. Can you hang on a sec?"

"Sure."

"Thanks." Curt pulled the phone away from his mouth and turned to his customer. "The terms are on the bottom there. One-third of the invoice must be paid when you drop the bike off, and the rest is due on completion of the job. Any questions?"

The guy shook his head. "Nope. Got it."

"Cool. I'll call you a few days in advance to make sure we're still all set."

"Awesome." He stepped toward the door then paused. "Hey, can I take a pic of the sketch to show my buddies?"

Anxious to take the phone call, but not wanting to be rude to a customer, Curt turned the pad around on the counter again. "Sure, just make sure my signature and business name are included."

"No prob. Thanks."

After taking a few quick photos, the guy left with a huge smile on his face. Curt brought the phone to his ear again. "Sorry about that, Dev. What's shaking in the security biz?"

"Not much. Listen, I just got back from a second trip to Belize and Kristen's having a really tough time this week with the morning sickness. I can't wait until it passes because she's been miserable. Little JD is being hell on his momma—"

"It's a boy? You found out?" He'd known that the parents-to-be wanted to name the baby John, if it was a boy, after Devon's younger brother, who'd passed away as a teenager. The kid's middle name would be his father's name, so John Devon was already being called by his initials.

"Yeah, two weeks ago. Polo has already warned me that JD and Mara are going to grow up thinking they're blood cousins because he's putting dating restrictions on the poor girl and she's only like, what, seven months old?" They both laughed before Dev continued. "Anyway, the reason I'm calling is this is my weekend to head up to Iowa with Archer, but I really don't want to leave Kristen when she's this bad. I'd ask one of the team, but they're all on assignments this week, even Jake. Is there any way you can swap weekends with me?"

"Actually, I already swapped with Archer. I meant to text you. But don't worry about it. When I spoke to Dana the other day to let her know I was coming in, she said things were low-key this weekend, so we were talking about taking the kids to that indoor amusement park or something. I can do that on my own...no biggie."

"You sure?"

He knew his friend felt bad. They usually took care of any teammate's widow for up to two years, depending on the situation, until she got back on her feet. They would still keep in touch after that, after all, they were family, but the bi-weekly visits would gradually turn to once a month before they eventually stopped. "Yeah, don't worry about it...got it covered. You just take care of your wife and that bouncing baby boy."

"Thanks. Oh, forgot to tell you. I'm sending you some business. One of the new Omega guys, Kip Morrison, has a hog for you to paint. He's a retired Army grunt, but we snatched him up from LAPD. I told him I'd hook him up with you."

"Sounds good. I'll be there in two weeks. Kristen called me about Kat's birthday party coming up, so I'll be crashing in the bunkrooms at the compound for the weekend." The woman was engaged to their friend Ben 'Boomer' Michaelson, and he was throwing her a party at the BDSM club the Trident team belonged to. Being good friends with Ian and his brother, Devon, both of whom owned the place, he'd been cleared to visit, but since he didn't want to deal with the medical clearances every six months, he didn't have play privileges. Not that he really wanted them anyway. To each his own. But damn, some of those scenes got pretty hot, and a few times he'd left with a serious case of blue balls. "I'll check out his ride then."

"I'll let him know. Thanks for the coverage and tell Dana I'll talk to her soon."

"Will do." He disconnected the call and tossed the phone on the counter. Letting out a heavy sigh, he ran a hand through his hair. When he'd agreed to take the shift for Pete Archer, he tried to convince himself he was helping out a friend by swapping, but the truth of the matter was he was dying to see Dana again. It had been two months since his last trip up there with Polo, and he found himself thinking about her all the time. He'd picked up the phone more times than he'd actually called her, but he forced himself not to hit the speed dial seven or eight times a day. And now he was going to be going there alone...well, not exactly alone—the kids would be there. Hopefully, they'd be reason enough to keep from touching her the way he wanted to. *Fuck!*

* * *

The non-descript sedan pulled into the drive, and Dana gave her reflection a quick look in the mirror, then silently chastised herself. The guys were coming for their twice monthly visit. This time, it was Devon and Curt. The latter had called her earlier in the week to let her know he was filling in for Pete. *He's not coming for you, you idiot. He's here because that's what the SEALs did—they did their best to fill the void in the lives of their fallen teammates' families.*

Dana knew she would have to tell them soon that she was ready to get on with her life without her husband. Eric had been her lover, best friend, the father of her children—her everything. It'd taken her weeks to finally admit to herself he wasn't on another tour of duty and would be home soon. Then it was months before she was able to get past the anger and hurt she felt—at both Eric and the bastard who'd hit him and left him lying on the asphalt like road-kill. But now, with the help of her family and friends, she was ready to come out of the darkness, which had shrouded her all this time, and start looking forward to the future. And a major step would be telling Eric's team they no longer had to visit twice a month. Phone calls and visits, to her place in Iowa or where the others lived around the country, would go back to the normal rate from before Eric's death.

Changing her mind about the lip gloss she'd pulled from the bathroom drawer, she tossed it back in and hurried out to the front door. She assumed Devon and Curt would be hungry after their flight and subsequent drive to Stormville, so she'd prepared some snacks for both the men and her children, who always seemed to be starving after school. But the kids wouldn't be home from school for another half hour, so the men got first dibs.

Not waiting for the bell to ring, she opened the door and stepped out on the porch. When she only saw Curt her eyes narrowed in confusion. "Where's Dev? I thought he was coming with you."

Hauling his military green duffel out of the back seat, he tossed it over his shoulder and started up the walk to the front door. "He called me Wednesday. Kristen has been puking her guts up with morning sickness. I told him not to worry about coming or getting someone to fill in since there wasn't much to do around the house this weekend. I hope that's okay."

Dana tried not to drool over the man she'd been friends with for years. When she'd started noticing him in a different way was hard to say. But somewhere along the line, she realized she was hoping the other guys would need someone to swap shifts because it always seemed that Curt was willing to do it.

As he climbed the stairs, she had to tilt her head back a little with each step. At six-foot-four, he towered over her by a good eight inches. Eric had been three inches shorter than his best friend, so with her heels on, she'd almost been on eye level with him. Curt was also a little broader in the shoulders, and over the years she'd heard many women comment on what an amazing physique he had. The two men had both been well built, but that was where the similarity ended. Eric had inherited his mother and grandmother's dark Italian genes while Curt's blonde hair and blue eyes had come from a long line of Norwegian DNA.

He stopped in front of her, and she realized she was staring and hadn't answered him. Feeling flustered, she turned to open the door. "Yes…it's…*um*…it's fine. Come on in."

When he followed and dropped his duffel in the foyer, it was then she realized he'd brought it in. He cleared his throat, catching her attention, and then scratched his head. "*Um*…I figured since it was just me, I could crash on the couch if it's okay with you?"

What? Shit, it wasn't like the man had never crashed on the couch here before. When they had first moved into Eric's childhood home, after his parents had retired to Arizona, she'd replaced the old couch with a sleeper sofa, which had an inflatable mattress for comfort just for Curt. He visited so often, she felt bad when he insisted on taking the couch, instead of letting her move one of the kids out there so he could sleep in a bed. But that was all before she was very aware of the man in a way she wasn't certain she wanted to be. "*Uh.* Sure. I mean, of course, you can stay here. If you want, Amanda can sleep with me and you can have her room."

21

He threw his head back and laughed, holding his hand to his gut. "*Ah*...no. Thanks, but all that purple and pink is too much for me. I'd probably smell like unicorns and be shitting glitter in the morning."

"Now there's an ugly picture." Dana shook her head, happy he sounded like Eric's old friend and not the man her body seemed to react to anytime he was near. "Come on into the kitchen. I bet you're hungry."

His boots barely made the slightest sound as he trailed her. It always amazed her how the big bad Navy SEALs could walk so quietly when there was no mistaking their presence when they were in a room. "It's not much. I just put out some cheese, pepperoni, spicy salami, and crackers."

"*Mmmm*. Now all I need is a beer, some pistachios, and a ballgame." Curt quickly made a small tower out of the spread she'd placed on the kitchen table and tossed it in his mouth. He chewed and swallowed while making another. "Much better than the six, damn pretzels I got in the package on the plane."

Knowing he wouldn't drink a beer at this hour unless it was at a barbeque or party, she retrieved a cold root beer from the fridge. She then grabbed a clean pilsner glass from the cabinet and set both on the table next to where he took a seat. Her ice water from earlier was still there, so she reached for it, but knocked it over when the house phone rang and startled her. Water and ice went flying right into Curt's lap. He leapt up, sending his chair sliding across the floor, but it'd been too late—the jeans on his crotch and thighs were soaked.

"Oh my God! Curt! I'm so sorry!" She lunged for a dish towel hanging on the oven handle and tossed it on the table where the water was still rolling over the edge to the floor. Grabbing another one, she reached to dry him off, but his hand snatched her wrist, stopping her.

He took the towel from her, as the phone still clanged on the wall. "I've got it. No problem. Answer the phone."

Sure he had things under control, she stepped around him and picked up the wall phone. "Hello?"

"Mrs. Prichard? This is Principal Gibbs at Stormville Elementary." Panic assailed her but he continued before she could ask what was wrong. "I'm sorry to call you, but I need you to come down to the school. I have Justin and Taylor in my office for fighting with two other boys."

"What?" Behind her, Curt froze at the shock in that one word. Her boys had never gotten in trouble for fighting before. "*Um.* Okay, I'm on my way. Is Amanda there, too, or did she get on the bus."

"She's on the bus. By the time I was alerted and stopped the fight, the buses had already started to pull away. Do you need to wait for her?"

Dana sighed. "*Uh.* No. I don't. A friend is visiting and he can get her. I'll be there in a few minutes."

After the man acknowledged her, she hung the headset back on its perch. She slowly turned around and found Curt eyeing her with curiosity. "That was the school. Apparently Justin and Taylor are in the principal's office for fighting."

"Each other?"

"No. Two other boys." She grabbed her cell phone from the table and her purse from where she'd placed it on the counter earlier in the day. "Can you get Amanda off the bus? It stops in front of Peggy Olsen's house. Ryan's bus will be about fifteen minutes later, but he can walk home on his own."

"No problem. I've got it covered. Should I do anything about dinner?"

Glancing around, she spotted her car keys on the small table in the foyer. "I'm just making spaghetti and meatballs. The sauce and meatballs are already made, so all I have to do is make the pasta later. Thanks."

She was about to turn for the door, but he put his hand on her elbow. His voice was gentle as his gaze met hers. "No thanks necessary, Dana. You should now that by now. I'm just glad I can be here to help out."

Biting her bottom lip, she wasn't sure what to say to that. There was something in his expression she couldn't quite zero in on. Certain her brain was misreading everything, she nodded. "I'm glad you are, too. I'll be back as soon as I can. Tell Ryan to start his homework, since we're going to the amusement park tomorrow."

"Got it. Go. I promise I won't burn down the house or let Ryan turn into a junior high school dropout while you're gone."

The smile that spread across her face was genuine. Curt had always been able to make her laugh...but now he was causing her to feel things she wasn't sure she should be feeling. Sighing to herself, she marched out the door. She needed to concentrate on her kids at the moment. Everything else would have to wait.

CHAPTER 4

"Uncle Curtsy!"

The little imp jumped off the bus and right into his arms. He hugged her, then lifted her onto his shoulders and strode back toward the house, waving goodbye to Dana's neighbor Peggy. Her husband, Phil, was a sheriff's deputy and Curt had hung out with him many times while visiting the Prichard household.

Eric's hometown in Iowa was pretty similar to Curt's own hometown in Montana. Both had less than twenty-five thousand residents and were an hour away, give or take a few minutes, from the closest major city. They were large enough where one didn't know everyone in the town, but if one of their own needed help, not only would the entire town come out in force, so would half the surrounding county.

"Where's mommy? She's going to be mad Justin and Taylor missed the bus again."

"Again?" He hadn't heard about this, so he doubted it was

anything of concern. He'd become Dana's sounding board at times when she was stressed. She had plenty of girlfriends, but they had their own kids and she felt bad about complaining to them. So he'd told her anytime she just needed an ear to bend, she should call him. Lately, though, it had gotten to the point he was kind of hoping the kids would get into trouble, just so she would call him and he could hear her sweet voice—pissed or not.

"*Uh-huh.* They missed it a few weeks ago 'cause they were playing catch. Mommy was mad."

"I bet she was." He lifted her down onto the porch and helped her get her pink and purple backpack off. "Well, I'm glad you didn't miss the bus because I'd still be out there twiddling my thumbs."

She giggled. "What's widdling?"

"Twiddling. Watch." He put his hands together and rotated his thumbs around each other. When she mimicked him, he grinned. "There you go. You officially know how to twiddle your thumbs."

Bringing her into the kitchen, he made a little plate of cheese and crackers for her since she didn't care for the meats on the platter. Then he retrieved the jug of sugar-free fruit punch from the fridge and poured her a glass. "So how was school?"

"Good."

"Learn anything new?"

She shrugged her shoulders. "Not really."

It amazed him that after six or seven hours a day in school, every kid he knew gave that same response. But then again, he'd probably been the same way when he was young.

A few minutes later, the front door opened and he tilted his chair on its back legs so he could see who it was. Another thing about small towns, it wasn't unheard of to leave your doors unlocked while you were home. He knew Dana locked it when it was just her and the kids, which was good. "Hey, Ryan. Mom will be back in a few. She had to go get your brothers at school."

The junior high school student dropped his bulging backpack with a thud and made a beeline for the fridge. Sticking his head in, he asked, "What? They missed the bus again?"

"Something like that." If Dana wanted Ryan to know what happened, it was her right to tell him. "She said for you to start your homework since we're going to the indoor amusement park tomorrow."

Ryan's head spun around so fast, Curt was surprised he didn't get whiplash. "Seriously?"

"Yeah!" Amanda cheered through fruit punch stained lips.

Uh-oh. Dana hadn't told them yet. He hoped it wasn't supposed to be a surprise that he just ruined. "Yay, but don't tell your mom I told you. She may have wanted it to be a surprise."

"No problem. I can fake being surprised, but I'm not too sure about short-stuff over there."

"I can fake surprise, too. See?"

Biting his lip to keep from laughing at the 'surprise' faces she was making, Curt couldn't help but see the little girl's father in her expressions. He'd never really noticed it before with her, but Ryan and Justin were the spitting images of their dad, while Amanda usually looked like her mom, just as Taylor did. A thought of what their child would look like if Dana and he had one together flickered through his brain. *Whoa. Shit. Where the hell did that come from?* Pushing it to the far reaches of his mind, he cleared his throat. "Anyway. Start your homework, so you don't have to cram it all in on Sunday."

Ryan shut the refrigerator door after retrieving a can of root beer and nothing more, before sitting at the table and making a few towers of meat, cheese, and crackers. Curt just shook his head. He'd had a perpetually empty stomach when he was a teen, and Ryan would be turning thirteen in about six weeks, so he hoped Dana was ready for the increase in food shopping.

"I'll get my history stuff done, but I'm leaving math until Sunday."

"What's the problem with math? I thought you liked it." The kid had always been a whiz at math, even at an early age.

"I like the math Mom teaches us. Not this core-math crap."

Curt gave him a sharp look. "Hey, watch your mouth. Especially around your sister." Eric would want his sons to know how to respect women, especially the ones they were related to.

The boy's gaze dropped to the table. His voice cracked as he apologized. "Sorry."

Oh, shit. He wondered if Dana knew her oldest son was starting puberty. He'd have to offer to teach the kid how to shave, now that he was noticing a little hair on his upper lip.

After stuffing his face, Ryan went to his bedroom to start his homework. In the meantime, Curt pulled Amanda's classroom folder from her backpack and left it on the table for Dana to look at. He knew the teacher put all announcements and assignments in it for the parents to keep track of since first graders had a tendency to forget or lose things.

With nothing to do but help Amanda with her homework, he opened the dishwasher, which had been running when he arrived, and put everything where it belonged. He listened as the little girl read out loud a list of three-letter words which all rhymed with 'cat'.

He'd just glanced at the clock and noticed it was almost five o'clock when he heard Dana's car pull into the drive. Moments later, she stormed into the house with two solemn looking boys in tow. Both were disheveled and Justin's shirt was torn. Slamming her purse on the counter, Dana ordered them through gritted teeth, "Go wash up and throw those clothes in the laundry, then start your homework. Dinner will be ready in an hour." As the two boys headed down the hall to their rooms, she turned to her daughter. "Amanda, sweetie, can you go play in your room for a little bit. I need to have an adult talk with Uncle Curt."

Uh-oh.

"Okay, Mommy." The girl closed her book and stood, but before she left the room, she ran over to hug her mother's hips. "Don't be mad. It'll be okay."

Dana sighed and squatted down to embrace her. "I know it will. Thanks, sweetie."

"You're welcome."

As soon as Amanda skipped out of earshot, Dana lost it. Pacing back and forth, she spoke low enough that the kids wouldn't hear her, but with plenty of venom. "I don't freaking believe that school. Un-freaking-believable. The two of them are suspended for three days, starting Monday, because they stood up to a pair of bullies who were harassing Justin's friend. Justin stepped in to tell them to back off and they both started in on him. Taylor saw what happened and ran over to help his brother. Once it was a fair fight, my boys kicked ass." She paused with her hands on her hips, then grinned. "Does that make me a bad mother that I'm glad they were the victors in the fight?"

Curt chuckled as he leaned against the table, out of her way. "Not in my book. Although, I assume no one was seriously hurt."

Pulling open the fridge door, she reached in for the pot of sauce and meatballs and placed it on the stove, then grabbed a clean pot from under the counter and began to fill it with water as she spoke. "No. Just a few scrapes and bruises on both sides. And Justin's ripped shirt. At least the principal suspended the bullies, too. I don't know the one kid, but the other one I'm not surprised about, since his mother is a bitchy bully, too. Of course, she's screaming she wants my ten-year-old and nine-year-old arrested for assault. Like that's going to happen. She's lucky I didn't need to be arrested for assaulting her. You have no idea how much I wanted to bash her face in." She put the water on the stove and then turned the dials for both front burners to heat the pots. "I feel bad for Connor though—the kid who was being bullied in the first place. He's Justin's best friend and he's got a physical disability. His hip was deformed at birth, so he walks with a pronounced limp—that leg is turned in a bit. The doctors want to wait until he stops growing before doing a hip replacement so he can walk better and be more active. It won't be a one hundred percent fix, but his limp will be dramatically less noticeable."

"That sucks."

"Yeah. And the thing that really sucks is he adored Eric and has been saying since he was five he wants to be a Navy SEAL, but you and I know that will never happen." She wasn't putting the kid down, but the BUD/s training for SEALs was so intense, very few men passed. With a limp, it was doubtful the kid would even be accepted into the military at all, no matter how slight the disability might be at that point. "I hope as he gets a little older, he'll find something else he dreams of doing which won't be hindered by his disability."

"I'm sure he will."

"Well, for now, I think that was part of why he was being bullied earlier. Telling everyone he wants to be a SEAL." She stirred the sauce, and then pulled a box of spaghetti from one of the cabinets. "And he's just got his mom. Dad was a deadbeat who left town before Connor was even born, so she's had it rough. I'm helping her plan his birthday party. She wants to make it military themed."

"She does, *huh*?" The wheels in his mind started spinning. His former teammates and he all had soft spots for kids, especially those who idolized the SEALs. "When's his birthday?"

"Two weeks from tomorrow. Why?"

He shrugged. "Let me make a few calls and see what I can do about surprising him with a few real SEALs."

Her eyes widened. "Really? I honestly didn't think of that. But I don't want the guys to fly in just for the day."

"Let me worry about that." He glanced at the clock, then pulled his phone out of his pocket. "I'll be right back."

CHAPTER 5

Stepping onto the back porch, Curt hit the speed dial for Ian Sawyer. While waiting for the call to be picked up, he surveyed the huge back yard. The only animals left on the farm were the chickens, but the old barn, which had once housed a few horses, pigs, and goats, was still there along with two storage sheds. Eric had wanted to begin getting farm animals again, like he'd grown up with, and had been getting the buildings usable once more when he'd been killed. Since then, they hadn't been touched except for the shed with the lawnmower and tool bench. The setup would be perfect for what he was planning, though, if he could get a few of the guys in.

The call connected. "Elmer. What's up?"

From the mild echo, he knew he'd been placed on speaker, which meant the man was probably still in his office. "Hey, Ian. Got a favor to ask, and since the six of you are the easiest way to get a group, I'm starting with you." He proceeded to fill his old teammate in on the kid's dream and how he wanted to surprise him.

"A SEAL birthday party, complete with SEALs, *huh*?"

"Yeah, I figure I could make a training setup in Dana's backyard, and we could use the laser tag weapons and show the kids how we do things. Then make them part of the so-called 'rescue' or whatever. I'll call Little Creek and have someone send me a bunch of Team Four hats and shirts, and I have some of our challenge coins we can give the kids. The only problem is his birthday party is two weeks from tomorrow. I can call around and see if anyone else can get in, but I figured I'd check with you first. I'll reimburse you for the jet fuel to fly up here."

"Fuck you, Elmer. Like I'm worried about that. But you're actually...sort of...in luck."

He could hear the other man typing on a computer keyboard. "Yeah? How's that?"

"Well, Parker and Shelby have decided to fly to Vegas to get married that weekend and we're all invited. Her sister's family just relocated there and Parker's disowned his, so instead of having a big to-do here, they want to do the Vegas thing. The team is flying up there with the women on Saturday, but the wedding is actually Sunday. We were planning on flying out of here around eleven or so in the morning, but let me see if everyone can leave the night before. We can stay at that nice hotel not too far from Dana's, then do the party around noon, if that's okay. That will still give us plenty of time to hoof it to Vegas afterward. It'll be easy to fly in and out of that local airport just outside of Stormville. All we'll need is a couple of SUVs or vans. Can you arrange that?"

"Yeah, of course. Are you sure about this, Ian? I know it's last minute and all."

"No worries. You know we love doing shit like this for the kids.

Let me check with everyone to make sure we can leave the night before and I'll call or text you back. Jake and Nick are meeting us in Vegas Saturday evening, though, because Nick has a training exercise scheduled for most of the day, so they're out."

"That's all right. Archer swapped with me, so he'll be here that weekend and so will Urkel." Steve 'Urkel' Romanelli was another former team member who lived just outside of Daytona. The man was a god on the basketball court and Curt had always made sure they were on the same team during three-on-three pick-up games because the guy was almost impossible to defend.

"Sounds good. I'll call you back later after I talk to everyone. I know the girls will be excited. They're all friends with Dana in that private SEAL wives and fiancées Facebook group and, according to my angel, they would love to finally meet her."

"I'm sure she'll love it, too. Talk to you later, and thanks."

Before they'd finished dinner, Ian texted him to let him know everything was a go from their end. Dana would call Connor's mom in the morning and tell her what they had planned. They would move the party to Dana's house, which wasn't a big deal since she had been helping with the arrangements anyway. Curt would then fly up two days early to get the backyard prepped for the SEALs vs. tangos showdown.

The cleanup from dinner went fast with everyone pitching in, then they pulled out a few board games and made an evening filled with laughter and fun. The domesticity and sense of belonging tugged at Curt's heartstrings. He'd wanted this thing—a family—for himself for a while know...even before Eric's death, but he hadn't found a woman with whom he wanted to spend the rest of his life with. And it never occurred to him the reason he hadn't was because he had to bide his time until the right woman was available. Was that woman Dana? He wasn't sure, but everything he felt during the evening seemed right...seemed perfect—except the ghost of a man who was in the room watching over them.

* * *

"Well, everyone's tucked in and excited about tomorrow," Curt announced as he strode back out to the living room where Dana had opened the pull-out couch and inflated the mattress. She was now in the process of putting the sheets on. Her back was to him as she bent over to pull the fitted sheet around one of the corners. His cock twitched, and he refused to let the groan in his throat come to the surface as he stared at her shapely ass.

"Great. I'm looking forward to it, too. I feel like I've been cooped up here forever." She grabbed the top sheet from where she'd left it on the recliner, unfolded it, and tossed it across the bed. He tore his eyes from her delectable body and picked up one of the two pillows she was giving him, stuffing it into one of the newly laundered pillow cases. "I figure we'll leave here at nine in the morning and, barring any heavy traffic, we'll be there by ten-thirty."

Dana finished tucking in the sheet and stepped past him to get the comforter from the back of the recliner. Her foot hit one of the boys' discarded sneakers and she lost her balance. Dropping the pillow he'd been stuffing, Curt's hands shot out to keep her from falling, and the next thing either of them knew, their bodies collided with each other. Chest to chest. Pelvis to pelvis. She gasped. Her soft body was flush against his hard one, including his erect cock, but he couldn't let her go. Her eyes grew wide as his shaft lengthened against her abdomen. The pulse in her neck picked up speed, and when her breath hitched he lost all reason and self-control. Lowering his head to hers, he waited

35

for the moment she would push him away and say no…but it didn't happen.

His lips met hers—closed mouth and soft. Just a brush of flesh against flesh. Electricity shot through him as the room around them sizzled. When her arms went around his neck and her eyes fluttered shut, he deepened the kiss. A little nibble. A little taste. He coaxed her lips to open with his probing tongue. When she obliged him, his hand went into her hair and held her head where he wanted it. As much as he wanted to devour her, he held himself back.

She tasted like heaven. A small shiver passed through her and he pulled her toward him, trying to do the impossible and imprint her body on his so he would never forget the first time he kissed her. They should stop…they really had to stop before one of the kids decided they needed to get out of bed and come out here for some inane reason. Just one more taste…one more lick…

Suddenly her body stiffened. *Shit.* She began to squirm and push against his chest. With reluctance but no regrets, he pulled away from her, yet still holding her in his arms. Her eyes were wide again, but this time in horror. *Damn it and fuck.* Her hand went to her mouth where her lips were moist, red, and swollen from their kiss. Her skin was slightly irritated from his five o'clock shadow.

Pushing him harder, she forced him to break contact. "I-I'm sorry…I just…I'm so sorry. I-I can't."

"Dana…" He reached for her, but she flinched, clearly not wanting him to touch her. Her eyes filled with tears and he watched helplessly as she fled to her bedroom, slamming the door shut. Curt's head dropped forward on his shoulders. He'd fucked up…big time.

* * *

Dana moaned and rolled over when her alarm went off. Eight a.m. *Shit.* She was exhausted, feeling like she'd only had a few hours of sleep. Well, then again, she had. She'd been up half the night after that...that...disaster, or whatever you wanted to call it in the living room last night. Kissing Curt...holy shit, what the hell had she been thinking? And what had *he* been thinking?

Then like a bawling teenager experiencing her first break up with a boy, Dana had run and hid in her bedroom. How was she going to face him today? It wasn't like she could avoid him since they'd be in the car together for three full hours. At least at the amusement park, he'd be taking the boys on the bigger rides, while she took Amanda and her friend, Nellie, on the slower and calmer ones.

Flipping the covers off, she trudged to her attached bath and turned the shower on before using the toilet. She stripped off the T-shirt, cotton shorts, and underwear she'd worn to bed, then stuck her hand under the spray to see if the hot water had kicked in yet. Finding it warm enough, she stepped into the tub and let the water drench her. After shampooing her hair, she grabbed the loofah from its hook beneath the showerhead. Squirting a quarter-sized dollop of her favorite bath gel, she washed from head to toe. But every time she touched her breasts and crotch, that old familiar ache grew stronger. She hadn't had sex since the morning before Eric had been killed, and up until recently it hadn't bothered her. However, her libido was finally making itself known again—like an awakening volcano, she might add—and she'd spent quite a few nights, alone in the big bed, with just her vibrators and memories. Lately, though, those long established memories had become dreams of the unknown...dreams of the man who was currently sleeping on her couch. At first, she'd been horrified, thinking of a man who wasn't her husband. But in one of her 'talks' with Eric, which she had whenever she needed his guidance, he'd given her his blessing to get on with her life. The only problem was, he hadn't 'told' her who to get it on with.

Was it wrong she was lusting after her husband's best friend…her *dead* husband's best friend? Some would say she'd mourned her loss long enough and it was time to get back to living once again. Others might say it was too soon, and she was only trying to replace her husband with someone familiar. So which group was correct? She didn't want to be lonely the rest of her life, but she also didn't want to risk losing someone who'd become more special to her than he'd ever been before.

She closed her eyes and dropped the loofah to the floor of the tub. Her mind drifted, conjuring up a chapter she'd read last night from Kristen Anders' new book, *Velvet Vixen,* when she'd been trying to get her mind off of Curt. While the BDSM lifestyle wasn't something Dana was interested in personally, Devon Sawyer's wife wrote a great combination of romance, sex, and suspense. Her books were fun and exciting reads, and the sex scenes were off-the-chart hot and steamy. But, of course, that didn't help Dana forget the man lying on her couch, a mere fifty feet or so from her bedroom door.

As she brushed one hand across her nipples, her other one drifted south to the juncture between her legs. If she was going to get through this day, being so close to Curt, then she needed to take the edge off her desire and confusion. She exposed her clit and gasped when one of her fingers slid across the top of it. *Oh, fuck this.*

Reaching up, she grabbed the wand of the shower head and unhooked it from the tiled wall. The dial could be turned to one of five different settings, and she knew exactly which one she needed right now—the fast, hard pulse option. The flow of water and hum changed and she pointed the makeshift sex toy at her throbbing pussy. Bending one knee, she propped her foot on the tiny corner shelf of the tub and threw her head back as the spray hit her in a way that made her hips thrust forward in need...and want.

While the water pelted her sex, she began to play with her nipples again. Rolling and tugging one and then the other. The pair of sensual assaults, combined with replaying in her mind the sex scene she'd read, resulted in her quickly climbing to the edge of release. Biting her lip, she aimed the pulse spray to the left just a tad and moaned when a jet hit a spot which took her one step closer. She tried to imagine what the fictional Master Zach looked like, but the only image her mind focused on was Curt's face...his hard body...his masculine hands on her feminine body...his low rumbling voice. *Cum for me.*

The orgasm that hit her took her breath away. Her legs almost gave out as wave after wave of pleasure came over her. She threw her hand out to the bar on the sliding glass door for support and it rattled...loudly. Letting go, she slapped the tile in front of her and tucked her face into her bicep to keep from screaming. Dizzy and sated, she slowly drifted back to reality, but worry settled over her. What if her attraction to Curt was nothing more than a fantasy? He'd obviously felt something for her last night. She'd felt the bulge in his pants the second their bodies connected, so he was sporting it before that moment. But what if there was nothing between them but sexual attraction? Could their friendship survive if they gave in to each other, only to find out the attraction was to be short-lived? She didn't want to lose him...and she didn't want her children to lose their father's best friend either—the man who could tell them all the stories only a few men knew about their dad. Stories of friendship, loyalty, laughter, brotherhood, and survival.

Shit. Eric, tell me what to do...please.

39

CHAPTER 6

Leaning against the kitchen counter, Curt took a sip of his coffee. Ryan was outside with Amanda, feeding the chickens and retrieving any eggs that'd been laid, which would be used for breakfast tomorrow morning. Today, the kids and he had all eaten cereal while waiting for Dana to shower and get dressed. After everyone was finished, he'd sent Ryan and Amanda out to the barn, and the other two boys to their room to make their beds and grab whatever they wanted to bring to keep them busy on the road.

He hoped Dana had slept well, because he sure as hell hadn't. When she'd fled to her room, he'd been tempted to chase after her, but knew it would be the wrong thing to do. She needed some time alone to think about what happened between them. He was as surprised as she was about the kiss, but she'd felt so right in his embrace that he hadn't been able to resist. For a full hour later, he could still feel her against him and taste her on his lips and tongue. He knew she'd been aware of the hard-on he'd gotten while eyeing her ass. It had been a normal male reaction to a woman he was attracted to, and it would've gone away on its own, had it not come in contact with her soft, feminine body. After that, all bets were off.

After tossing and turning on the couch until midnight, he'd known if he was ever going to get any sleep, he would have to take matters into his own hands, which he'd done in the shower. Imagining her on her knees in front of him, sucking him off, it hadn't taken him long to shoot his load into the shower spray. And damn, just thinking of her now, was making his dick twitch.

Down the hall, he heard her bedroom door open, so he retrieved a clean mug from the cabinet and was pouring her coffee as she entered the kitchen. The dark circles under her eyes told him she hadn't slept any better than he did. "Good morning."

She took the steaming mug he handed her, bringing it to the table where the milk carton still sat next to the sugar bowl. She avoided looking him in the eye. "Morning."

"The kids are all fed. Ryan and Amanda are out collecting eggs while the other two are in their room. Do you want cereal or something else?"

"No thanks. I'm not hungry. I'll just drink this and bring a granola bar with me for the road."

"Dana…" He grabbed her elbow and tried to turn her to face him, but she pulled out of his gentle grip. Still refusing to look at him, she began to put away the boxes of cereal and milk. Curt had already placed the dirty bowls and spoons in the dishwasher.

"Can we not talk about this now?" At least they were both thinking about the night before, but whereas he wanted to discuss it, she clearly did not. "I would rather we both forget it happened."

Stepping toward her, he boxed her in by placing his hands on either side of her hips as she spun around in surprise. "Look at me." He waited, but her gaze was pinned to his chest. "Damn it, Dana. Look at me." Slowly, she tilted her head back until he could see her eyes. "What if I don't want to forget about it? What if I've been dreaming about kissing you for weeks now?"

She brought her hands to his chest and tried to push him away as she shook her head, but he wasn't budging. "Please. Not now. I-I think it was a mistake."

"And I don't." The sound of Ryan and his sister climbing the back porch stairs had him taking a giant step away from her, but his eyes never left hers. "We will be talking about this later. For now, though, I'll drop it so we can have a fun day with the kids. But don't think for one minute I regret kissing you."

Before she could respond, the back door opened and Curt pasted on a tense smile, which quickly became relaxed and real as he listened to Amanda chatter about how many eggs they'd found.

* * *

A little after seven-thirty that evening Curt carried a sleeping Amanda from the couch into her room and tucked her into her bed. The cute pixie was exhausted from all the fun she'd had during the day with her friend and family. Closing her door behind him, he passed Justin and Taylor in the hallway, yawning on their way to their room. Ryan was already in his own bedroom on his Xbox. It wouldn't be long before the entire house was sleeping soundly from the long day. But before that happened, Dana and he were having a talk about the kiss, whether she wanted to or not. He had to let her know he was interested in taking a forward step to a closer relationship with her, but only if she was ready. He wouldn't push, but he also wouldn't wait forever. Patience may be a virtue, but even the most patient man on earth had a breaking point.

Returning to the living room, he saw it was empty. From the sound of things, Dana was cleaning what he already knew was a spotless kitchen. Sighing, he picked up a heavy throw blanket from the back of the couch and strode into the kitchen where she was scrubbing down the table she'd wiped down that morning before they left. Placing the blanket over her shoulders, he pulled her upright.

"W-what are you doing?"

"We're going to sit out on the porch for a little bit and talk," he told her, taking the damp sponge from her hand and tossing it across the room into the sink.

"Curt, I can't. I have cleaning to do."

Steering her toward the back door, he gently pushed her forward, his hands cupping her shoulders. "The house is spotless, as always, to the point I'm wondering if you're a little obsessive about cleaning. It won't fall down if you leave a crumb or two on the table." He reached around her and opened the door. "Outside…please."

Huffing, she grasped the edges of the blanket and pulled it tighter around her body. Following her out the door, he pointed to the bench swing when she leaned against the railing. "Please, sit with me. I promise—all I'm going to do is talk and hold your hand. Nothing more."

The wariness on her face deepened, but she didn't argue. Taking a seat, she got as close to the armrest as she could, trying to keep as much distance between them as he sat next to her. He rolled his eyes and took her hand in his, resting them on his thigh. "I'm not going to attack you, Dana. Please, relax."

Using his foot, he started the seat swinging. He gave her a few minutes for the tension to ease from her body as he stared out at the darkened mountain, which started its incline sixty or so acres from where they sat. Brushing his thumb over the back of her soft hand, he took a deep breath. "Do you know what I first thought when you were walking toward our table that night at The Clamshell?" He didn't wait for her to respond, nor did he look at her. "I was kinda pissed Eric had seen you first because I would've loved to have hit on you." Beside him, she snorted in disbelief. "No, really. It's true. You were smokin' walking across the bar. Every guy was checking you out, not just me. Then I got to know you and saw how much Eric was in love with you...I think it was love at first sight for him. I'd never seen him as nervous as he'd been with you. It was like he knew already that you were 'the one' and he didn't want to fuck it up.

"I was more than happy to have you as a friend...there were plenty of other women out there and I wasn't the kind of guy who would hit on a friend's girl. You became like a sister-in-law to me...note I said 'in-law'. You could never be a sister to me. A guy like me doesn't have dreams of a woman he considers a sister. I didn't have them often, just every once in a while. I kinda felt guilty about it, but since I would never act on it, it wasn't a problem."

He finally turned and faced her, even though she was still looking out over the vast universe as if it held all the answers. "I can't deny my feelings have changed, sweetheart. At first, I thought it was because I promised Eric I would watch over his family if anything ever happened to him." She knew all about the vow he'd made many years ago. "But then those dreams started coming almost every night. You're not just a friend to me anymore. I force myself not to call you every day, just to hear your voice." His gaze returned to the horizon. "Hell, the last time I had sex with a woman was over a year ago—"

"Get out of here, Conrad Michael Bannerman. Don't give me that. You date all the time."

Chuckling at her incredulous tone and use of his full, given name, he shook his head. "No, I'm dead serious. And, yeah, I *used* to date all the time. I'll admit it. I was a man-whore during my twenties and the first half of my thirties. But then I realized I wanted what you and Eric had…a family…someone to grow old with. I started going out on dates looking for 'the one', but none of the women were her…now I think I know why. I wasn't looking for just any woman…I wanted a woman like you. Someone who made me laugh and let me crash here anytime I wanted to visit…no questions asked. Someone who made sure I had somewhere to go for every holiday. A woman who worried if I was eating right, or booked a flight for my best friend to fly to Daytona when she heard I crashed my bike and was in the hospital." That had happened a few years ago and that's exactly what Dana had done while Eric had been on the phone with Curt's brother trying to get updates. Curt had broken a few ribs and his arm, along with having a major concussion for which they'd put him in a medically induced coma, but thankfully, he'd completely recovered. He'd awoken four days later, when they'd eased him off the meds keeping him asleep, to find Eric sitting in a chair, anxious to make sure he was all right.

"Look. I know this is difficult territory for us…I'm sure you're worried about the kids and what would happen if things didn't work out…but, sweetheart, I can't help but think this is the start of something beautiful between us. Something that was meant to be. Not years ago…but now. Just promise me you'll think about it. I won't bring it up again until I come back up in two weeks. Then, if you want to leave it as friends, I'll abide by your wishes. But just know you're special to me, more now than ever, and I've never wanted another woman the way I want you." Yeah, that was dirty pool, attaching that on at the end, but he hoped it would lead her to start having dreams of the two of them together. Why should he be the only one taking cold showers like the one he needed right now?

Dana remained quiet for a few moments, clearly pondering all he'd said. The silence didn't bother him, instead, he found it comforting. He continued to swing the seat, content to just sit there beside her. He wasn't sure how much time passed before she shifted a little closer to him. Letting go of her hand, he put his arm around her and tucked her into his side.

"I promise I'll think about it…about us."

She paused and he thought she wasn't going to say anything more, but then, with a sharp intake of breath, she rested her head on his shoulder. "I meant to tell you, it looks like I'll be going back to teaching next school year."

He smiled. This was familiar ground they'd stepped back on—chatting about everyday things. "Really? Wow, that's great."

She'd been working as a high school math teacher when she'd met Eric all those years ago. After they'd married and Ryan had arrived, followed by Taylor, she'd become a stay-at-home mom until the kids were old enough to go to school. Her tutoring a few students after school had supplemented Eric's military pay. But then Justin and Amanda had followed, and they'd all moved to Iowa when Eric retired from the SEALs. He'd put his combat experience to good use, working for a company that trained men and women to be bodyguards. Not the Hollywood type of guards, but the ones businessmen needed when they went to foreign countries where it wasn't uncommon for Americans to be kidnapped for ransom. A retired SEAL from Team Two had started the business about ten years ago in Texas, and Eric had contacted the guy about opening another training facility about a half hour south of Stormville. The franchise had been a success and was still operating with a new boss at the helm.

"Yeah. It's time. The extra life insurance money Eric took out won't last forever, and I need to start working again, if only for my sanity. One of the teachers is retiring at the end of the year at the high school, and I applied for the job when I heard about it. They called me yesterday morning and told me the position was mine if I wanted it. Ryan's not thrilled since he's got one more year before he starts ninth grade, but at least, he won't be assigned to any of my classes."

Figures. Most kids wouldn't want their mother teaching in the same school they attended. "I'm sure he'll get over it."

"Probably."

She shivered and he tightened his hold on her. Although the temperature was dropping and they would have to go in soon, neither one of them made an effort to stand. What he wouldn't give to have this time with her every night.

CHAPTER 7

Eighteen Months Ago

After he finished taping the parts of a bike that weren't being painted, Curt stepped out of the ventilated stall as his cell phone rang on his hip. He was usually out somewhere on a Saturday night watching a ball game or sometimes just vegging at home, but for some reason, he'd been uneasy all day. Unable to describe the feeling or figure out what was causing it, he couldn't shake the sense that something wasn't quite right. To get his mind off of it, he'd taken his bike for a ride to the shop and started prepping the new custom order for its paint job on Monday morning.

The phone continued to ring as he tossed the roll of trimming tape onto the workbench. It was probably Eric calling him back. While Curt had been at the gym earlier, his buddy had left a voice mail saying he needed to talk to him about something, and to call back as soon as he could. Curt had gotten the message after retrieving his duffel bag from his gym locker, and left his own message on Eric's voice mail when his friend didn't pick up.

Plucking his phone from its belt clip, he glanced at the screen. *Dana.* That wasn't odd. She called him at least once a week. She probably forgot to tell him something when he spoke to her yesterday morning. Connecting the call, he brought the phone to his ear. "Hey, sweetheart. What's up?"

"C-Curt…"

His body tensed. "Dana, what's wrong?"

Her words came out in a rush. "He didn't come home. I don't know what to do. It's been three hours. I called—"

"Slow down, sweetheart. Slow down." That feeling he'd been having all day intensified. "Who didn't come home? Ryan?"

"No. Eric." She took a deep, trembling breath. "He went out for his run three hours ago. I don't know where he is. His cell went to voice mail."

What the hell? He'd just assumed it was their oldest son she was talking about and Eric was out searching for him. That kid always lost track of time. "Do you have anyone out looking for him?"

"Phil Olsen is driving around trying to find him. Curt, I'm scared. This is so unlike him. I have this feeling something happened to him and I don't know what to do."

A heartbreaking sob came across the line, and it twisted his gut. There was no way Eric would worry Dana unnecessarily like this, and that just made the situation even more troubling. "All right, listen. Call Phil. Tell him to make it official with the sheriff's department and get every out looking for him. I'm going to call Ian and see if his pilot can fly me up there."

"You-you don't have to do that."

49

"Yes, I do. If you hear anything, call me right away." After she acknowledged him, he hung up the phone and hit the speed-dial button for Ian, then started locking up the garage while he waited for the call to connect.

"Sawyer."

"It's Curt. We've got a problem."

He filled his former teammate in and requested the use of their company jet. It would be the fastest way for him to get up there and join the search. Some people might say it was only three hours since the guy went missing, and to wait awhile. But in his heart, Curt knew something was seriously wrong and he needed to be there when they found out what it was.

When Ian asked if he wanted anyone from the team to go with him, Curt replied, "No. I have no idea what's going on, but I do know the people in that town and the sheriff's department come out in droves when someone is missing. If we need more help, I'll call you."

"You're sure? I can move things around."

"Yeah. But Ian, man…I've got a bad feeling about this."

"So do I. I'll have the pilot waiting for you at the municipal airport. Call me as soon as you land and have info."

"Will do…and thanks."

Three and a half hours later, the private jet landed and Curt found a sheriff's vehicle waiting for him. He was grateful for the lift since the rental car agencies in the small airport were closed for the evening. As Deputy Phil Olsen drove, he filled Curt in on what was happening. There were dozens of law enforcement personnel, firemen, and volunteers out looking for the missing husband and father, but with the darkness of the night, they'd failed to find any sign of him so far. "The last place anyone can confirm he was spotted was about twenty minutes or so into his run. One of our neighbors was driving through town and passed him going the other way on Main, just west of Bluebird Drive. We haven't found anyone else who may have seen him after that, but at that time of the evening it's dinner time for most folks around here. Eric varied his routes all the time, so we can't figure out exactly what roads he took and where he was heading. From Main and Bluebird, there are way too many side streets he may have taken, or continued out to County Road 32 or turned left into the county park to run the trails."

The deputy had barely stopped the car in the Prichard's driveway when Curt leaped from the vehicle and rushed up the walkway to the front door. Finding it unlocked, he entered and, after a quick glance in the empty living room, strode toward the kitchen where he heard low voices. He hoped like hell he'd find Eric had returned within the last few minutes and it was all a misunderstanding they would laugh about. But seeing Dana, her eyes swollen and her cheeks stained with tears, his hopes were dashed. Ryan and Phil's wife, Peggy, were sitting at the table with her. When Dana saw him enter the room, she jumped from her seat at the dining table and ran into his arms. "Thank God you're here. There's still no sign of him."

Her body trembled as he hugged her tight. "We'll find him. I promise you." What he didn't add was 'alive or dead'. But he knew with each passing hour, the chances of finding Eric Prichard alive and well were diminishing. The man would never walk out on his family, he wasn't suicidal, and from what Phil had told him on the way over, he'd left his wallet and credit cards behind. They'd tried pinging his cell phone, but it was either off or the battery was dead, and the last calls or texts he received had been before he left the house.

Dana gave him a squeeze, then stepped back. The look in her eyes was a combination of fear and determination. "You bring him back. I trust you to bring him back to me."

He knew right then that she feared the worst had happened...the same feeling Curt was fighting in his own mind and gut. But until they heard otherwise, he'd tear the county apart until he found his best friend.

"Uncle Curt, I want to go with you." Ryan stood and approached him, worry etched on his eleven-year-old face.

Biting his bottom lip, Curt grasped his nephew's shoulder and pulled him near. He leaned down so they were face to face. "I know, buddy, but I need you to stay here and look after your mom for me, all right? I need to know she's in good hands. We have a lot of people out there looking for your dad and we're going to find him. Understand?"

The boy's eyes, so much like his father's, blinked back a few tears and then he nodded. "Okay."

"Good boy." He turned back to Dana. "Can I have the keys to Eric's truck?"

She snatched the spare set of keys off a hook next to the phone on the wall. "Of course."

"Where are the rest of the kids? In bed?"

Shaking her head, she put an arm around Ryan, who was obviously taking his new assignment seriously and sticking close to his mother. "No. Amanda's staying at her friend Nellie's house and Justin and Taylor are up the street, sleeping over at a friend's house. They don't know what's going on...I didn't know what to tell them."

Curt ruffled Ryan's hair and kissed Dana's forehead. "All right. Let me hook up with the sheriff's department and find out where they've searched and what areas still need to be covered. Call me if you need me."

"Just bring him home."

Another wave of dread passed over him and he gave her a somber nod. "I will."

Fourteen hours later, Curt found his best friend. Eric had been struck by a vehicle and thrown into a cornfield on the side of County Road 32. Volunteers had passed the area several times, but it wasn't until Curt and several deputies walked along the road that he noticed what the others had missed. Pieces of a recently broken headlight, with what looked like blood smeared on them, were found on the grassy shoulder. Eric's battered body was located about twelve feet into the rows of corn and hadn't been visible to those driving past.

Now, the deputies were keeping Curt from disturbing the hit-and-run crime scene as they waited for the medical examiner to respond. The sheriff was making sure the news didn't reach Dana until Curt returned to the house to tell her himself. It was his duty and he wouldn't pass it off to anyone else.

He paced back and forth on the dirt shoulder opposite from where his buddy lay. How long? How fucking long had Eric laid out of sight as his life faded away? Did he know what was happening? Did he suffer? Could he have been saved if someone had seen it happen? *God damn it!* He was in the middle of bum-fuck Iowa, where he should have been safe. They had survived countless missions together in some of the most dangerous places on Earth, and Eric fucking buys it on the side of the road in fucking Iowa, of all God-damned places. "Shit."

Wishing he had something or someone he could hit, Curt strode back to Eric's truck, climbed in the driver's seat, and slammed the door. Anger and sorrow coursed through his veins, as he pounded his fist on the dash. "Son of a fucking bitch, Eric! It wasn't supposed to be like this, you asshole…it wasn't fucking supposed to be like this."

He took a deep breath and ignored the wary look on a deputy's face as the man walked past the truck on his way to his patrol car. Shoving his outrage back down to deal with later, Curt pulled his phone from his pocket and hit the speed dial button on his phone for Ian.

"Talk to me, Elmer."

Fighting the quiver in his voice, he told his friend and former teammate they had to bury one of their own.

* * *

The next two days flew by in a blur. Eric had always said he didn't want to be waked at all. He hated them. Dana and best friend knew they would only be planning a funeral, followed by a party…not a morose reception, but a fucking party. He'd wanted everyone to celebrate his life, not mourn his death. Family, friends, and Eric's Navy brethren began arriving in droves on Monday while Curt escorted Dana to the funeral home to make all of the arrangements for Tuesday's service. SEAL Team Four was stateside and those who could boarded a flight to Iowa, along with a Navy honor guard for the gravesite service after the mass at the family's church.

Curt stood by Dana's side throughout the entire ordeal. He'd been a godsend for her and the children. After barely getting through the funeral without falling apart, they invited everyone to attend the 'celebration' at a local pub Eric and Curt liked to go to for a beer and a ballgame every once in a while. There were many men dressed in their formal Navy blue uniforms mixed in with the civilians. It was a testament to the brotherhood Eric had belonged to.

"Can I have everyone's attention, please? Listen up!"

Dana glanced up from cutting Amanda's chicken fingers into little bits. Ian Sawyer was standing on a small stool so he could be seen by everyone in the place. At the bar next to him, Devon, Brody, Marco, Jake, and Boomer were helping the pub owner and bartender with a case of Jameson's whiskey. She knew what was coming, having attended several SEAL funerals in the past. There would be two toasts. The first one included everyone—family, friends, and teammates. The second would be later on, reserved for Eric's brothers-in-arm only. It was a team tradition which had started a long time ago and was repeated, without fail, at every Team Four funeral.

There were a bunch of whistles and shouts of 'quiet' before the crowd of one-hundred-plus people hushed. With the help of the waitresses, dozens of plastic shot glasses filled with whiskey were passed out to everyone over the age of twenty-one. For the minors and those who didn't drink, a few were filled with cola, so they could still participate.

Bringing a small tray of shots over to the table, Curt made sure Dana and her kids had the appropriate drinks. As the glasses were passed to those who hadn't received one yet, Ian took the one Devon handed him. "For those of you who don't know me, I am proud to say I served with Eric for many years—it was a privilege to have him on my team. We have a tradition on our team to toast the fallen with a whiskey tribute, and I invite you to join us for the first one. His teammates will have another one later, in private. As the ranking retired officer here, I was asked to lead you in this first toast. Does everyone have a glass?" When he was certain all had received one, he lifted his own in the air. "Eric Prichard. Call sign, Wabbit. It was your team's honor to serve with you and to call you our brother. Your loyalty to your country, your team, your family, and your friends will never be forgotten. You served your country with honor and integrity, the same way you lived your life. Today, we saluted you and then your fellow SEALs proudly slammed our tridents into the top of your casket as a sign of our undying gratitude and respect. Your family is our family and we will always be there for them since you no longer can be. Take care, my brother, until we meet again."

There wasn't a dry eye in the place when all the SEALs shouted out '*hoo-yah*' before they downed their shots.

A little over an hour later, most of the local folks had left, and Dana was saying goodbye to those who remained. Her mother and Jenn Mullins were gathering up the children so they could all head back to the house. Jenn was Ian's goddaughter, and her father had been on Team Four, as well. The team had watched her grow since she'd been a baby and she called a lot of them 'Uncle'. Her parents, Jeff and Lisa, had been murdered six months ago, and Jenn was just beginning to emerge from her dungeon of angst. She now lived with Ian in Tampa, while going to college nearby. The sweet girl had been entertaining the kids all day, and Dana was grateful.

Scanning the room, she saw Curt talking to Marco while drinking another soda. She knew he was staying sober so he could help her, but she was worried about him. He hadn't broken down yet, trying to be strong for her, and she knew it was only a matter of time before his grief hit him square in the chest. She wanted that to happen while he had his teammates around to watch his back.

Spotting Ian and Devon chatting a few feet away from her, she stepped over to them. Ian lifted his arm around her shoulder and pulled her into his side. Placing a brotherly kiss on her forehead, he asked, "How are you doing, Dana?"

"As good as I can be at the moment, but I need you to do me a favor."

"Name it."

She sighed. "I'm going to be heading home in a bit with my kids and the grandparents. Jenn is coming, too, for a little while. Can you make sure Curt stays here with you, please?" Devon raised an eyebrow at her, but she continued before he could ask any questions. "He needs you guys right now. He's been a rock for me since he got here, but I can tell he's holding back. Get him drunk and watch his six…do what you guys do for each other at times like this. You can drop him off later—he's been crashing on the couch. Even though they're coming back to the house for a while, my mom and in-laws have been staying at the bed-and-breakfast in town, and the kids will sleep like rocks tonight. Just call my cell phone when you're on your way and I'll open the door."

"Are you sure?" Ian asked. "We can throw him in a bed at the hotel. No big deal."

Shaking her head, she glanced over at the man in question. "No. It's okay. Bring him to the house. He's staying the rest of the week to help me with all the paperwork with the V.A. and other stuff. You can pick Jenn up, then, and bring her back to the hotel."

"We'll take good care of him. I promise. And if you need anything, you have most of our numbers, right?"

"I do." She swallowed a sob that wanted to burst forth. "Thanks…for everything. I…I couldn't have gotten through this without all of you here."

Ian pulled her into a full hug, wrapping both arms around her. "That's what we're here for, sweetheart. Eric was a brother and we take care of our own."

"I know you do."

CHAPTER 8

It had been a long day, and it was far from over. Curt hoisted five-year-old Amanda up into his arms when she came over to him while he was talking to Polo. As she rested her head on his shoulder, he told his friend about Eric's last phone call. "It sucks. I missed his freaking call and by the time I got the voice mail, it was too late. His cell had been in his pocket and was smashed. That's why we couldn't ping it. The weird thing is, he sounded worried about something."

Marco took a swig of his beer. "What'd he say?"

"Just that he really needed to talk to me and to call back as soon as I could. Dana doesn't know what it was about. I don't know...maybe I'm trying to figure out why it happened. It was probably some effing drunk..."

"Uncle Curtsy? What does effwing mean?"

Rolling his eyes as Marco chuckled, Curt gave Amanda a squeeze before setting her on her feet once more. "Nothing, sweetie. I think Jenn is looking for you over there." He pointed to where the young woman was gathering the children's jackets and Amanda's coloring book. "Why don't you go help her, okay?"

"Okay."

He watched as she skipped away, then spotted Dana who was making her way over to him. When she reached him, he put his arm around her. "Everyone is starting to head out. Do you want to go to? I'll start saying my goodbyes real quick and then drive you home."

Placing her hands on his broad chest, she shook her head. "No. You stay here with the boys." He opened his mouth to argue with her, but she cut him off with a few taps to the medals over his heart. "I know you all have another toast to do. Jenn is coming back with me along with my mom and Eric's parents. I asked Ian to drive you back later and then he could pick up Jenn. I'll be fine."

He let out a heavy breath and realized he was surrounded by the Trident Security group and a few others in full uniform. Not only were his former teammates here for Dana...and Eric...they were here for him too. Ian nodded at him. "She's right. We have another toast to do, and that one is all yours, my friend. Let's get drunk and rowdy and have some laughs in Wabbit's honor. He wouldn't expect anything less from us, and you know it. Since Dev doesn't drink, he's going to make sure everyone gets home safe later."

Swallowing the lump in his throat, his gaze returned to Dana. "I still have the keys to Eric's truck in my pocket and the house key is on it, so lock up if we're not back by the time everyone goes to bed. Tell Jenn to crash on the couch, if she wants until we get there."

"Got it covered, Elmer." He smiled because it was rare she used his call sign. "I'll leave a few bottles of water and some Tylenol on the coffee table. Take them before you pass out."

That was Dana. Always making sure everyone else was taken

59

care of…especially him. He hoped someday soon he found a woman who was just like her, because when he did, he'd make that woman his wife.

Fifteen minutes later, the pub owner turned on the lights to a small party room in the back of the restaurant for the SEALs to continue the celebration of their buddy's life. They would be out of the way, and view, of the dinner crowd which would start filing in soon. Ian had arranged for the daytime bartender to stay on. A little corner bar in the room was stocked with a variety of different beers on ice and about a two dozen bottles of Jameson's. They would need at least that much for the fifty or so retired and active SEALs present. A few wall mounted TVs were turned on to several sports games with the volumes off. Music was piped in from the main bar area, but it was low enough to just be background noise.

As the shots of whiskey were being passed around once more, Curt focused on what he was going to say for the toast. The first one had been devoid of vulgarities, as clean as an admiral's dress whites, for the sake of the family and children. However, this one was for the men who had trained, sweat, and fought side by side with their fallen brother—cursing wasn't only expected, it was a requirement.

Once everyone had their whiskey, they turned to face Eric Prichard's best friend. All backs in the room were ram-rod straight and each set of shoulders squared in honor of every drop of blood shed. Curt had to clear his throat several times. There was a reason, aside from the cursing, why this toast was done in private—tears were sure to flow and men like them preferred not to cry in public.

Taking a deep breath, Curt lifted his glass high above his head. His gaze was on the ceiling as he spoke to Eric in the great beyond. "Wabbit, you son of a bitch. We walked through hell together, and blew fucking smoke up the devil's ass. We rocked a lot of women's worlds and a lot of their beds, too. Big tits, small tits, we squeezed them all, my friend. But then you met your beautiful wife and, not long after, your kids came along. Your brothers will lay down their fucking lives for your family, so rest assured we still have your six. Hang tight, brother Wabbit, until we meet again. Then we'll all let fucking loose and blow smoke up a few angels' skirts. *Hoo-yah!*"

"*Hoo-yah!*"

* * *

Present

"They're here!" Justin shouted as the three packed SUVs pulled into the drive. He ran from where he and the other boys had been waiting in a section of the backyard, where they could see the vehicles come down the road, to the front of the house. His five other friends, plus the birthday boy, Connor, were hot on his heels. While the kid's limp was noticeable, he had spunk and tried not to let it limit him.

Curt did a final scan of the makeshift training area in and around the barn, then slapped Ryan on the shoulder. "Thanks for the help. You did a great job."

The boy grinned with pride at him. "It was fun. I can't wait to shoot some tangos."

They had spent most of yesterday and the entire morning setting up bales of hay, which Curt had arranged to be delivered, and other objects to make places to hide behind and use as cover while searching for the bad guy. Pete Archer and Steve Romanelli had flown in early yesterday morning to help, since the Trident team hadn't been able to take off from Tampa before seven p.m. last night, due to a few things that couldn't be rescheduled. They had all gone straight to the hotel when they arrived and Curt had met them there for a quick beer.

The other men and he wandered out to the front yard. The Trident team had brought plenty of toys for the day of SEAL games. Obviously, none of the weapons were real, but they were incredible simulation training tools. It would be a cross between high-tech laser tag and real life war games.

Ian climbed out of the driver's seat of the first vehicle as everyone else scrambled out. His fiancée, Angie, stepped forward and gave Curt a hello kiss on the cheek. Glancing around, he greeted everyone else who had come—Devon and his wife, Kristen, whose baby bump had started to show. Boomer and his girlfriend, Kat. Brody was solo this time. Ian and Devon's cousin Mitch was there, along with Charlotte Roth, a.k.a. Mistress China from the BDSM club the cousins owned. While not involved in the security business, the two were attending the wedding as well, and Curt had invited them to the party with everyone else.

Marco was the last one Curt spotted and he had his arm around his woman, Harper. Yeah, that had been a shock. The day after they'd had that conversation back in January when Marco had repeated his old mantra about never having a wife and kids, the guy's life had flipped upside down. He'd found out he was the father of Harper's little girl, who had been born at the end of last summer. Because of some whack job's interference, Marco hadn't known about his daughter, and Harper had been led to believe he wanted nothing to do with either of them. Curt was glad to see everything had worked out between them because he couldn't remember ever seeing Polo so happy. From what Curt had been told last night, little Mara was home being babysat by Harper's mother and Jenn Mullins, who was also dog sitting Parker and Shelby's dog, Spanky. The twenty-year-old had a big exam coming up during the week in one of her classes at University of Tampa, and she wouldn't have been able to enter the casinos anyway, so she'd opted to stay home.

After the men greeted the children, who were in awe of being surrounded by U.S. Navy SEALS, they unloaded all the gear and carried it to the backyard. The women had zeroed in on Dana since this was the first time they were meeting her in person. Curt hadn't realized how close they'd all gotten to her via Facebook. Bringing them to where picnic tables had been set up just off the back porch, she introduced them to several of her friends who'd come to help with the party.

As Curt grabbed one of the last duffel bags, another SUV pulled in. This one had a light bar on the roof and 'Caution—Police K9' on the rear windows. Both front doors opened and Phil Olsen hopped out of the passenger seat. The driver was the Sheriff Department's K9 handler, Sean Kilduff, who had volunteered to bring his dog, Kilo, and give the kids a show of what his partner could do. Phil would be donning the protective attack suit for the demonstration.

Once everything was set up, Ian handed out Team Four T-shirts and baseball caps to all the kids, including little Amanda and her friend Nellie. The birthday boy, Connor, was grinning ear-to-ear as he put them on. Then the men took some of the grease paint they'd brought, and smeared it on the youngsters' faces, with their parents' permission of course. Might as well go all out and make the kids feel like they were really on a secret mission.

Brody was off to the side helping Boomer get into his high-tech gear to be the bad guy. The jumpsuit and ski mask he was putting on would register any hits from the laser guns. Each weapon showed up in a different color, so they could tell who hit where. Back at the

Trident compound, they had a hollowed out building with movable interior walls to change the setup. The walls, ceiling, and floors were coated with special black paint which would show the heat from the laser shots for about fifteen minutes until fading away. It was all really cool, and Curt loved joining the team for some training runs every now and then.

Grabbing Amanda, and then Nellie, under the arms, he hoisted them up on the bed of Eric's pickup truck, which they'd used to bring all the bales of hay into the backyard. "All right, gang! Listen up!" He made sure he had all the kids' attention. There were eleven in total—the two girls, Ryan, Taylor, Justin, Connor, and the five other boys. Curt pointed at Ian dressed in his black cargo pants, boots, and a grey T-shirt. "That man right there? He's your commander. You can call him Lieutenant, Boss-man, or sir. You *will* listen to everything he says and you *will* follow his orders. Give him a big 'yes, sir'."

Grinning, the kids all shouted, "Yes, sir!"

Ian clapped his hands together, then waved everyone into a huddle which included the back of the pickup so the girls didn't have to get down. "All right, team. First, we're going to talk safety. It's extremely important in combat. Number one—you always point the muzzle of your gun at the ground until you're given the go order."

"How come?" one of the boys asked. Curt couldn't remember his name at the moment. "You said they don't have bullets in them."

"That's right." Ian pointed at the youngster. "Good question. We train that way because sometimes we use real weapons and sometimes we use the fake ones. You don't ever want to mistake one for the other in the heat of the moment, so you treat every gun as if it's the real thing. You never aim a gun, fake or real, at anyone you

64

don't intend to shoot. Got it?"

The boy nodded. "Yup."

"Okay. Next. Our bad guy, or tango, over there..." He tilted his head toward Boomer. "...is going to hide somewhere in the barn. If it's not your turn, no giving away the tango's location if you saw where he went. That's poor sportsmanship. Whoever's turn it is, you're going to team up with Elmer here. He'll walk right behind you and point out where you need to go. When you see your target, aim and shoot. Got it?"

The kids shouted in unison, "Got it!"

Taylor raised his hand. "Lieutenant Ian, who goes first?"

Taking the ball cap Urkel handed him, Ian showed them it was filled with folded pieces of paper. "Since it's Connor's birthday, he gets to go first. Everyone else will go in the order their names are pulled. Fair enough?" They agreed. "Okay. Hand signals." He held his fist at shoulder height. "This means stop and stay where you are. No talking until you're given the all clear. I'll point where I want you to go. We'll keep it simple with those two signals. Elmer, get Connor ready. The rest of you can watch from the door on the other side of the barn or up in the loft, so you're out of the way, but can still see everything. And remember...no giving away the tango's location."

While the other kids scrambled to get a good observation spot, Curt gave Connor a crash course on how the gun worked. It was pretty simple—there was a safety switch, sights, and a trigger. If it wasn't for the fact it was painted red for safety reasons, the assault rifle looked and felt like the real thing. Because the boy's arms weren't long enough for the stock to rest against his shoulder, Curt instructed him how to hold it, point, and shoot.

When everyone was set, a four-man team consisting of Connor,

Ian, Urkel, and Brody closed in on the target building, using trees and the bales of hay for protection as they leap-frogged forward. Curt coached the boy on how to cover his teammates when they were moving out in the open. The team waited patiently as Connor limped from spot to spot. Soon they reached the large opened barn door with Connor, Curt, and Urkel on one side of the door frame and Ian and Brody on the other side. Ian signaled Egghead to enter and provide cover for the others. He then pointed with his finger for the birthday boy to enter and search for the tango.

With Curt's hand on his shoulder guiding him, Connor moved from stall to stall searching for the tango. He found Boomer hiding in the third one on the left and fired his weapon. Of course, the former SEAL had to get dramatic, clutching his chest and performing one of the worst death scenes ever. Cheering, Connor's teammates high-fived him, and the kid was on cloud nine. This is why the men loved to do shit like this with children...to see that mile-wide smile.

One by one, the kids took their turns on the search and destroy mission. Even the deputies, Phil and Sean, took turns, then the former suited up in the attack suit and they gave everyone a show of Kilo's abilities as an aggressive tracking dog. After he'd taken the 'bad guy' down, the K9 was rewarded with his favorite Kong toy. It always amazed Curt how dogs trained for military and law enforcement could switch their aggressiveness on and off with a verbal command. When Kilo wasn't working, the big Belgian Malinois was a mush, just like Trident's trained dog, Beau. That dog loved his large, human family, which was steadily growing.

By three p.m., the Trident team and their women and friends were all packed and they said their goodbyes before heading to the airport. Curt handed out the SEAL Team Four bronze challenge coins he'd brought with him for the kids. They were collectors' items, and the only way you could get one was from a current or retired member of the team. Challenge coins got their start in the Air Force during WWI. A wealthy pilot had some made for his squadron as a token of their service. Over the years, the idea spread and they were now very popular throughout the service. Some were easier to get than others.

After making sure everything was cleaned up, Urkel and Pete headed back to their hotel. They told Curt if he wanted to join them they were going to go the pub where Eric's repast had been for a few beers and dinner. He declined, but made plans for them to come back to Dana's for breakfast before heading to the airport for their own flights home. One to Colorado, the other to Florida.

The rest of the parents attending, mostly women, had helped clean up the food, cake, and birthday decorations and they all thanked Curt for making the arrangements for a party their kids would never forget. Connor and his mother, Susan, were the last to leave. The boy threw his arms around Curt's waist until he squatted down so they were eye to eye. "Did you have a good time?"

"It was the best! I can't wait to tell everyone at school I was a SEAL for my birthday!"

Curt ruffled the boy's hair. "And you have the pictures to prove it." The Trident team usually avoided pictures, which might end up on the internet, for security reasons. But with the black grease paint and the brims of their ball caps pulled low to obscure their faces, they had joined in the group photo. After the pictures were taken, they'd all cleaned off their faces with baby-wipes.

When he stood again, Susan stepped forward and hugged him as well. "I don't know how I can convey how much this meant to both of us. You're an angel."

Blushing, he glanced over to where Dana was watching and gave her a wink. He then took a step back and grinned at Susan. "I think I know a few terrorists who will disagree with you, but I'm glad we were able to make Connor's birthday special for him."

"Oh, you did! Not sure how I'm going to top this next year, though." They both laughed and then the woman led Connor and Justin, who was going with them for a sleepover, to her car.

Dana stepped over to where Curt was waving goodbye as they drove away. She gave him a teasing hip check. He chuckled then gave her one in return.

"Ya know, Elmer? Ya done good."

He let out a bark at her statement and put his arm around her shoulders as they walked to the backyard. It was something Eric had said often after a successful mission or when praising his kids for a job well done. "So, now what do we do? Amanda's spending the night at Nellie's. Justin's gone, too. Want to see if the other two want to go see a movie later, or what?"

"I think they would love to go, but would you mind if I stayed home?"

Stopping, he turned to face her. "Everything all right?"

"Yes. Fine. I'm just tired. It's been a busy few days. In fact, I'm surprised you're not ready to pass out."

"Are you calling me old, woman?" Reaching out, he tickled her sides, eliciting a squeal from her. She then pivoted and made a beeline to a tree to try and hide behind it, but he was right on her heels. Grabbing her around the waist, he lifted her off the ground and spun in a circle, sending her legs out in the air.

"Curt! Put me down!"

Her laughter belied her indignation. But when he spotted Taylor and Ryan watching them, he thought it best to stop and take his hands off their mother. They weren't used to seeing a man other than their father teasing and holding her. Dana hadn't told him her decision yet, but he was determined to have it before he left on Monday. He'd planned for an extra-long weekend because, honestly, he had no desire to return to Daytona. Every time he left her and the kids now, a little more of his heart stayed behind. Now, he just had to hope Dana would, one day, want him to stay.

CHAPTER 9

After making sure Taylor and Ryan were in the latter's room playing X-box, Dana took a deep breath and headed for the back porch where Curt was having a beer. It was just after nine p.m. and she knew she'd procrastinated long enough. She knew the boys would be occupied until they went to bed, so she didn't have to worry about them. It was time to take a leap of faith.

Passing the refrigerator on her way, she grabbed a bottle of Bud Light for herself. She rarely drank at home, but tonight she needed a hint of liquid courage. She opened the back door and stepped out into cool night air. They'd lucked out with the weather for the party, and the temperatures had been in the low seventies. Not bad for the last weekend in April. But now it was cool enough for the sweatshirt she'd thrown on over her V-neck tee.

Curt was sitting on the porch swing as he'd taken to doing in the evenings, just staring out at the woods surrounding the several acres Dana owned and the mountains in the distance. His head turned when he heard her open the door and he moved over on the seat to make room for her. "Didn't think you were going to join me."

"I was just finishing a few chores and making sure the boys were settled." She sat beside him and took a sip of her beer as he put the swing in motion.

Not knowing where or how to start the conversation she knew he was waiting for, she let the silence drag on for a few minutes until Curt let out a weary sigh. "Your answer is no, isn't it?"

"What? No! I mean, no, my answer isn't no." She shifted and brought her knee up on the seat so she was facing him. His eyes were wide with surprise. "I just...I want to take this slow...I mean...God, what do I mean?" He remained silent as she untangled the web of thoughts in her mind. "I'm attracted to you, Curt, there's no denying that. More than I ever expected to be with you or anyone else after Eric. But I have to think of the children. While you and I figure out if this is what we both want, we need to keep it from the kids...at least for now. I don't want them to think you're replacing their dad or get the impression we have a future together, only to be disappointed if it doesn't work out."

He nodded. "I completely understand and agree." A seductive grin spread across his face and she felt herself grow wet. "So, for now, we have to sneak around and hide if I want to steal a few kisses from you. I kinda like that. It sounds naughty."

Oh, hell, when he talked like that, all she wanted to do was jump his bones. He must have had a similar thought because he took her beer and placed it with his own on the little table next to the swing. Standing, he held out his hand and when she took it, he pulled her up. Hand-in-hand, she followed him as he led her to the barn. The big sliding doors on either side were closed once again, so they entered through the small, pedestrian door. He flipped on a switch which turned on one overhead light only, so they could see, but left the others down the length of the building off.

Dana was nervous as hell, but she was also dying of anticipation. Her body had been craving this man's touch for weeks now. Stopping at the bottom of the ladder which led to the loft, Curt turned to her and cupped her face with his hands. "I'm going to kiss you, now, sweetheart. No one else is around. It's just you and me. I'll stop if and when you want me to, but no running away."

His voice was husky and mesmerizing as she stared into his soft brown eyes which were bright with desire. All she could do was nod and lick her lips, silently inviting him to take what he wanted. Lowering his face to hers, ever so slowly, his lips touched hers and sparks flew. One of his hands went to the back of her head to hold her in place as the other slid down her back and pulled her close. Her arms snaked around his neck as she went up on tippy-toes.

The kiss was gentle at first, almost hesitant, as if they were both expecting the other to back away. But then Curt grew bolder and used his tongue to encourage her to part her lips for him. When she did, he turned her and backed her against the wooden ladder. Her hands went into his hair as he consumed her. Their tongues dueled with each other and he ground his pelvis against her abdomen. It wasn't enough for her—she was too short for him to rub his erection where she wanted it the most.

Putting one hand on his chest, she pushed until he broke the kiss. He was as breathless as she was. "What? Are you okay?"

Instead of giving him a verbal answer, she nodded then turned around. Placing her hands and feet on the ladder, she climbed up into the loft, then looked back down at him. Giving him a coy gesture with her finger for him to follow, she grinned when he practically flew up after her. Dana quickly found the sleeping bags which were stored up there with the rest of the camping equipment. With Curt's help, she opened and spread out three of them on top of each other on the wooden floor, wishing they had some of the bales of hay to make it softer.

As he took her hand and pulled her down on their makeshift bed, there was a moment of trepidation which passed through her and he must have sensed it. Sitting with his back to the wall, he lifted her onto his lap. "Sweetheart, listen to me. We don't have to do anything but cuddle and kiss right now. No matter how much my cock is jabbing your hip." She laughed as he waggled his eyebrows at her. "But seriously. We'll take this as slow as you want to go. I just don't want you to have any regrets afterward."

Her heart opened to him a little more. Was it possible to fall in love with two men in a lifetime? *If Eric was still alive...no...do not go there. He's gone. Your love for him will always be there, even if he can't be. But that doesn't mean you can't fall in love again— especially with the man who has become your best friend over the past year.*

Taking a deep breath, she reached up and skimmed her fingers along his jaw, which was covered with coarse stubble. She brushed her thumb over his plump bottom lip and his tongue darted out to taste her. Leaning in, she replaced her thumb with her mouth, groaning as he began to ravish her as he'd done moments before. She was hungry for him. Shifting, she straddled his hips. His hands settled at her waist as if he were letting her take the lead. But she didn't want that. She wanted them to be equal in this.

As she rubbed against him, chest to chest, she felt him harden further at the juncture between her legs. He pulled down the zipper of her sweatshirt and she yanked it off her shoulders and arms, tossing it aside. His hands slid up on either side of her rib cage, just under her heavy orbs as he lifted them, feeling their weight. Bunching up his T-shirt in her hands, she tugged it from his pants. When he leaned forward, away from the wall, she pulled it up and over his head. Her gaze dropped to his sculpted pecs as she glided her fingers over them. Wanting…no…needing to be skin to skin with him, she grasped the hem of her shirt and removed it before reaching back and unhooking her bra. She was desperate for his touch and didn't care if it showed.

Through heavy-lidded eyes, he watched her remove her clothes. The lust she saw there mirrored her own. Rising up on her knees, she brought her breasts to the level of his mouth. Her pussy clenched in need when he pulled her closer and his lips latched on to one nipple as his fingers played with the other. A gasp escaped her when he flicked his tongue over the stiff peak. Holding his head to her chest, she reveled in the sweet torture he was lavishing on her. He began to alternate between the two breasts, sucking and licking one, while teasing the other with his fingertips.

Dana's head fell back on her shoulders as she tried not to cry out how good it felt to be touched by this man. He left her breasts and twisted his torso until she was lying flat on her back. Following her down, Curt took her mouth once more as he covered her body with his own, holding the majority of his weight on his forearms at either side of her shoulders.

His pelvis met hers and he ground them together, making her moan and beg as he nuzzled her neck. "Please. Naked. Need to be naked with you now."

She reached down for the fly of his cargo pants, but he slid down her body, out of her grasp. "*Uh-uh.* You first."

Kissing her abdomen, he undid the button of her jeans and lowered the zipper. He tugged at the denim and Dana lifted her hips to help him. Yanking the jeans off her legs, he threw them aside and ran his hands up her calves and thighs. His eyes were zeroed in on her plain white panties, and she silently cursed herself for not wearing something prettier.

Spreading her legs wider, he crawled forward and inhaled deeply. "Damn, your scent is the sweetest perfume. I wish I could bottle it."

How the hell did he make her wetter just by giving her a compliment? Curt lowered his mouth to her mound and she gasped when he blew hot air through her panties. His hands slid back up to her breasts, kneading the flesh and flicking her nipples with his fingers. Her moaning grew louder as her eyes fluttered shut. She squirmed underneath him, her breath increasing and her pulse racing. "Oh, Curt. Yes…oh, God, yes!"

"Say it again, sweetheart. Open your eyes and say it again."

Her hips bucked, needing him to put his mouth back on her. "Yes!"

He nipped the inside of her thigh and her eyes flew open. Her gaze met his intense one. "Say my name again, Dana."

She knew what he meant…what he needed. He had to make sure it was just the two of them in the barn…in the moment…and not the ghost of the dead man they'd both loved in different ways. "Conrad Michael Bannerman, if you don't rip off my underwear this instant and put that mouth of yours to better use, I'm going to go insane."

Chuckling and smirking, he grabbed the white cotton fabric and pulled, shredding it from her body. Dana let out a quick squeak. "That's not what I meant!"

"Too bad. Now, what was that second part again? Something about putting my mouth to better use?"

He didn't wait for an answer from her, instead attacking her pussy with fervor. Flattening his tongue, he dragged it up her slit, over and over again. He ate her like a starved man, feasting on her swollen pussy lips. His hands seemed to be everywhere at once as he took her higher and higher. Chin stubble rubbed against her inner thighs.

"Oh, shit! Curt! Please!" She clutched his hair, the silky blond strands tickling her fingers. One of Curt's hands trailed down her abdomen and stopped right above her mound. His thumb brushed against her clit and her hips bucked. "Oh! Oh, God! Don't...don't stop! Oh!"

Bringing his mouth to her sensitive bud, he sucked while dropping his hand further. One finger, then two, eased into her core and she felt another rush of fluid escape her. Her grip on his hair tightened, but it didn't seem to bother him as his assault picked up speed. Plunging his fingers in deep, he curled them, searching for the spot which would push her over the edge. Dana was just shy of hyperventilating, gasping for air as her body prepared to explode.

"Cum for me, baby. Let it go."

His order sent her soaring. She bit her bottom lip to keep from screaming at the top of her lungs as her body quaked with the force of her orgasm. His mouth was on her again, as she came for him. He drank her, licking and swallowing every drop, and it sent her over the edge again. She squirmed to get away, to get closer, to...damn, she didn't know what she wanted, but it wasn't for him to stop.

As she returned to Earth, his tongue rasped her slit a few more times before he lifted his head and their gazes met. Her eyes were almost closed but she could still see him. "That was better than I dreamed it would be."

Grinning, he wiped her cum from his chin and cheeks. "Really?

So you *have* been dreaming about me. Good to know." He went up on his knees, his hands going to the pockets of his pants and his face plummeted. "Shit, baby. My wallet is back in the house. I don't have any condoms on me and I don't suppose you're on the pill, are you?"

Ah, shit. Wide-eyed, she bit her lip and shook her head. "No, I'm not. Sorry."

He sat back on his heels and rested his hands on her calves, rubbing his thumbs over her skin. "Don't be sorry, sweetheart. It's my fault, but maybe it's a sign to take things a little slower. I meant what I said before—I don't want you to have any regrets in the morning."

"I won't." Her gaze dropped to his crotch where his bulging cock was very noticeable. Her mouth watered. "Maybe we could take care of that in another way."

Curt groaned and his head fell forward on his shoulders. "As much as my dick would love that, baby, I'm going to say no. I want the first time to be inside that delicious pussy of yours and if I have to wait, I'll do it." His eyes met hers again, the intensity there burning into her soul. "But be forewarned, I'm buying a case of condoms because I have a feeling once I get inside of you, I'm never going to want to leave. I'm going to fuck you ten ways to Sunday, then come back for more. Now, before I forget I'm an honorable man, get dressed and go back to the house. I'll follow after I get rid of this hard-on."

As she sat up, he leaned forward and brought his mouth down hard on hers. She tasted herself on his lips and tongue, and it sent her body into overdrive again. When he pulled away and stared at her, she could see his reluctance and knew he wanted her as much as she wanted him. He rolled over onto his back as she stood and got

77

dressed, sans the underwear he'd shredded and now held in his hand. Watching every move she made through half closed eyes, he licked his lips and brought her panties to his nose. She faltered as he inhaled her scent which was lingering on the fabric. The sensual act caused her pussy to throb again.

"Hurry up, sweetheart, before I forget every reason why I'm sending you back to the house, instead of fucking you silly."

Heaven help her.

CHAPTER 10

"Honey?"

Sitting at the kitchen table, paying her bills online, Dana glanced over her shoulder at her mother-in-law, Alice. Jeff's parents had flown in yesterday to attend the wedding of a friend's daughter this weekend and were visiting the grandchildren while they were there. The couple was sleeping in Amanda's room, with the trundle bed pulled out, while the six-year-old slept with her mother. Forty-eight hours from now, it would really be a full house when Curt arrived on Friday for the weekend. "Yes, Mom?"

The woman, who was a second mother to her, sat beside her. "I know it's a school night, but I was thinking that you and I could go to dinner at Claire's tonight. Earl can order pizza for him and the kids. Is that okay with you?"

A night out without the kids sounded like heaven right now. Sunday had been miserable with Taylor suffering from a stomach virus which had him puking the entire day. She'd put him in her bed, then she slept in his so his roommate, Justin, wouldn't catch it.

Curt and she had barely had a minute alone with all four kids home and needing to finish up their homework. Ryan had been in a crabby mood for the past few days and Dana was at her wits end. It wasn't until Curt pointed out to her that her oldest was starting puberty she realized this was what her life was going to be like with one or the other kids for the next few years. "It's more than okay with me. Thanks."

Alice patted her hand then stood again. "Good. I'll tell Earl he's on babysitting duty for a few hours."

After her mother-in-law left the room, Dana's cell phone alerted her to a text. Her heart rate sped up as it did every time her phone rang or chimed since Curt had left on Monday morning. He'd cut it close with his departure to catch his plane, but he'd wanted to kiss her goodbye properly—his word—before heading to the airport, and they'd had to wait until the Ryan left for his bus stop. The elementary school bus the rest of them took was usually fifteen minutes earlier than his for the junior high. Taylor had stayed in bed for most of Monday, recovering from his virus, so they hadn't worried about him seeing them.

Picking up her cell, she read the text.

Missing you, sweetheart. Hope you have a great day. Will call you tonight – Me.

She quickly typed a response saying she missed him, too, and for him to call later than usual because she was going out to dinner with Alice. Finishing up her bills, she shut down the laptop then went to her bedroom to shower and change. After closing the door, she glanced around the room. Her heart clenched. There was so much of Eric still in their private sanctuary, how could she bring Curt into the bed she'd shared with her husband? It wasn't just

Eric's picture, but the little things she hadn't had the heart to put or give away. His valet with the gold watch she'd given him upon his retirement from the SEALs sat on the high-boy dresser. His kindle was still on what had been his nightstand, the battery drained to nothing a long time ago. She'd donated most of his clothes to charity, but saved some of his favorite T-shirts to sleep in, just to feel close to him.

Sighing, she pushed all that from her mind and began to get ready to go out to dinner. Two hours later, Alice and she had placed their orders at the little restaurant they both loved to eat at when they got a chance. A few minutes of idle chit-chat and a glass of wine had Dana relaxing, but then her mother-in-law changed the subject.

The petite, black-haired woman sat back with a smirk on her face. "So...do you want to tell me who's been calling and texting you and has you smiling so much this week, or do I have to play twenty questions before I can make an educated guess?"

Dana's jaw dropped and she froze. Had she been that obvious? How the hell was she going to tell her mother-in-law she had feelings for a man, who wasn't her son, only a year and a half after Eric died.

"Oh, honey, don't look so shocked. Earl and I knew that someday you might fall in love again and it doesn't mean you loved Eric any less. Who is it?"

Taking a sip of wine, Dana hoped Alice wouldn't be too surprised with her answer. "Well, honestly, it sort of came out of the blue. Neither one of us was expecting anything to happen and we're taking it slowly because of the children..." She knew she was babbling, but when she glanced at the other woman's face, all she saw was love and delight. "It's Curt."

Of all the things she expected from her mother-in-law, it hadn't been her clapping with glee. "Oh, I was hoping you were going to say that." She then reached across the table and took Dana's hand. "I think Eric would give you and Curt his blessing, honey. And Earl and I certainly do. If any man was as honorable and kindhearted as my Eric, it would be Curt. Every time the two of them came to visit, he treated us as if we were family, and we felt the same way about him. And when they were leaving, Curt would always hug me and say, 'Momma P.? I will lay down my life for your son. That's how much he means to me. You raised a great man.'"

Her eyes filling with tears, Dana grabbed her napkin and dabbed at them. "Yeah, that sounds like him. But are you really sure it's okay?"

"Aren't you?"

Sighing, she tried to put into words what she was feeling. "Yes, I'm attracted to him, very much so, and he's become my best friend over the past year..."

"But..." Alice made a 'continue' gesture with her hand.

"But I'm worried about the kids. How they are going to take it? Are they going to think I'm trying to replace their dad? What will other people think? Is it too soon? And, well...this is kind of embarrassing, but I know you and I can talk about this stuff. I'm scared to bring Curt into the bed I shared with Eric. You probably think I'm crazy—"

"Stop it, Dana." The woman's stern expression and tone had her snapping her mouth shut. "Okay, first things first. The children. Yes, in the beginning, they may think Curt is trying to replace their dad, but talk to the school psychologist—I'm sure she will be able to give you pointers on how to approach them with it. Next. What will other people think? Who the heck cares? Many years ago, a friend of mine passed away. Mary and her husband were a match made in heaven and he was devastated when she died suddenly from a stroke at the age of thirty-two. At a grief counseling group, six months later, he met a woman who made him smile again. Twelve months later they were married and still are after thirty-some-odd years. Only you know when it's right, and to hell with everyone else."

Dana smiled, her heart feeling lighter than it had since Curt had left on Monday. Afterward, she'd started having all these doubts again, but her mother-in-law was dispelling them in one conversation.

"Now, about that last issue. The bed. I'll tell you what we'll do. You know Eric had taken out a small insurance policy for us, in addition to the one you had. Earl and I have never touched that money—we were leaving it to you and the children. You and I are going furniture shopping tomorrow at that next-day-delivery place and we are getting you a new bedroom set."

Her mouth couldn't drop any further if it tried. "I-I can't ask—"

Alice held up her hand. "Please. Let us do this for you and Curt. You're the daughter I never had, Dana. It would mean a lot to me to see you happy once again." When Dana just nodded because she was too choked up to respond, Alice grinned and patted her daughter-in-law's hand before leaning back so their waitress could put their plates down. "Good. Now, let's eat and have a wonderful evening."

* * *

Curt hugged Eric's mother then turned to shake Earl's hand, but the slightly shorter guy pulled him into a man-hug. "We meant what we said, son. I hope it works out for you and Dana because you both deserve to be happy. We know you loved Eric and would never do anything that would harm his wife and children."

He swallowed the lump in his throat. He'd known the couple had arrived earlier in the week to spend some time with Dana and the kids, but when he'd gotten there himself a few short hours ago, he hadn't expected the greeting they'd given him. Somehow they had figured out Dana was interested in someone after all this time and they'd hoped it was him. The wedding they were going to was an hour away, so for the next two nights they were staying at the hotel where it was being held, and then heading straight to the airport on Sunday. "Thanks, Pop. It means a lot to me that you approve."

"We were always as proud of you as we were of Eric. You're a good man, son, and I couldn't ask for a better one to look after my grandchildren. We'll be coming back up the week after the fourth of July for another wedding, so we'll see you then. Take care."

Curt clapped the man on the shoulder. "You, too. Have a good time at the wedding and call when you arrive at the hotel, so we know you got there okay."

"Will do."

After Alice finished talking with Dana a few feet away, she turned and gave him one more hug and a kiss on the cheek. "Love you."

"Same here, Momma P. Always."

Dana and he waved as the couple drove away, then he put his arm around her shoulders. "Well, I didn't expect that."

She snorted. "Neither did I." Taking his hand, she tugged him toward the front door of the house. "You won't believe this either."

His eyes narrowed in confusion, but he still followed her willingly. "What?"

"You'll see." He was surprised when she led him to her bedroom and was even further shocked when she opened the door. "Alice and Earl insisted on getting me a new bedroom set..." She turned and her gaze met his. "They knew I was going to have a hard time bringing you into the bed I shared with Eric, so..." She shrugged and gestured to the new, solid oak bed, night tables, dresser, and highboy. "They were delivered first thing this morning and I paid the delivery men to deliver the old set to this couple I know from church who just got married, but don't have much money to decorate their place. I asked Father Jaffe to arrange it."

Grinning, Curt placed his hands on her hips and pulled her to him. "How much time do we have before the kids get home?"

Dana chuckled as she ran her hands up his arms and locked them behind his neck. "About an hour. What did you have in mind, Elmer?"

"I figured we could get started on the case of condoms I brought with me."

"*Hmmm*. Sounds good to me. Shall we break in the new bed?"

He backed her up to it, then tightened his hold on her hips, lifted and threw her onto the bed as she squealed. "You read my mind."

Digging his wallet out of his pocket, he tossed it on the nightstand after removing one of the three condoms he'd stuck in there. Call him optimistic. He grabbed her ankles and dragged her toward him. First, he removed her sneakers and socks, then tugged

85

on her jeans when she undid the snap and zipper. They didn't have much time so he began to remove his own clothes with zeal, starting with his T-shirt. "Take the rest off, honey."

He licked his lips when she shed her shirt and bra as he shucked his pants to his ankles, stepping out of them after toeing off his boots. Dropping to his knees, he tucked his hands under her thighs and brought her to the edge of the bed. Her skin was silky smooth as he kissed his way up to her wet and inviting pussy. "You have no idea how many times I got hard as a fucking rock thinking about how you tasted the other day. Reach down here and spread these lips wide for me, baby. I want you to hold yourself open for me."

His nostrils flared when she didn't hesitate and he breathed in her womanly scent. Damn, he really wished he could bottle that. Dipping his head, he ran his tongue up her pink slit, eliciting a moan from her. He sucked on one swollen lip and then the other before stiffening his tongue and impaling her with it.

"Oh, shit! Curt!"

"Finger your clit, sweetheart. Show me how you got yourself off while you were on the phone with me." Monday night, long after the kids had gone to sleep, the two had gotten into a hot and heavy phone sex session. Curt couldn't remember the last time he'd done that with a woman, but with Dana, he planned on making it a regular occurrence.

Replacing one of her hands holding her open with his own, he licked her again as her fingers made circular motions over the tiny bundle of nerves above her pussy. He slid two fingers into her soaked sex and fucked her in time with the pace she set on her little clit. When she sped up, he sped up…when she slowed, he slowed. He grinned when she realized what he was doing and she picked up the pace again. Sliding his other hand up her body, he took a nipple between his two fingers, pinching and pulling it.

Overcome by the combination of sensations, Dana gasped and bucked her hips. Her fingers worked her clit furiously as he plunged his fingers into her core over and over again. "Curt! Oh, God! Harder! *Ah...ahhhhhhhhhh*, sssshhhhhhhit!"

His fingers and hand became drenched with her cum as she plummeted into an orgasmic abyss. He didn't let up his assault on her pussy as she screamed for him. Replacing her fingers on her clit with his mouth, he prolonged her pleasure as long as possible. Her walls clenched and quivered around his fingers and he couldn't wait to shove his throbbing cock in her. As she drifted back down, he grabbed the condom package from the nightstand and ripped open the package. He didn't waste any time rolling the latex over his sensitive, hard flesh.

"Move back, sweetheart." After she used her feet to propel herself into the middle of the bed, he crawled over her body and settled between her widespread legs. Lining himself up with her slit, he fought the urge to just thrust in with abandon. Being it had been such a long time since either of them had had sex, he eased into her, using short strokes to advance further and further until he was buried to the hilt. Closing his eyes over how snug she was, he held himself still until she adjusted to his length and girth. When she began to squirm beneath him, he lifted his hips, pulling part of the way out, then plunged back in. The drag of his cock against her walls was pure heaven and it took everything in him to wait until she began climbing the cliff to coital bliss again, taking him with her.

"Harder, please, harder!"

Who was he to deny her request? Fucking her hard and fast, he felt her walls begin to spasm again and when her orgasm overtook her, he roared his own release as she milked every drop of cum from him.

Spent and gasping for air, he remained deep inside her and felt the last of her tremors fade away. They were both covered in a sheen of sweat, but neither cared as he dropped his forehead to hers. It was only then he realized he hadn't kissed her mouth yet. Tilting his head to the side so their noses were out of the way, he brushed his lips against hers. "I don't know about you, but for me, that was well worth the wait."

Wrapping her legs tighter around his waist, she clenched her pussy surrounding his softening cock. "Definitely worth the wait. But now I can't wait to do it again."

Lifting his head, he glanced at the bedside digital clock then smirked at her. "Well, we do have another half hour before the kids get home."

CHAPTER 11

Sitting at the kitchen table, sketching a new bike design which had come to him, Curt's head whipped around at the sound of one of the cabinets slamming shut. Scowling, Ryan opened the refrigerator and grabbed a deli bag of sliced turkey. He continued to open drawers and cabinets, retrieving what he needed to make an after-school sandwich, all the while creating an unnecessary racket.

Curt studied him for a few moments, before finally asking, "Something you want to talk about?"

The boy ignored him and slammed the fridge door shut again.

"Talk to me. Maybe I can help."

"Maybe you're the problem."

Okayyyy. Not what he'd expected. "Why am I the problem?"

Ryan spun around and crossed his arms. "What are you doing here again? Mom said she told Ian the SEALs didn't have to come all the time anymore."

Curt was stunned at the venom in the boy's voice and tried to figure out where it was coming from. Nodding, he stood and leaned against the kitchen table. "She did. At Connor's party. Most SEAL families stop the visits when they've gotten through the worst, a year or two after a death. We all expected your mom had reached that point."

"So what are you doing here? We don't need you anymore."

"Ryan!" Both of their heads turned at Dana's shocked exclamation as she stood in the doorway to the hallway. "Apologize to Curt this instant."

"No!" he shouted. "I don't want him here! The only reason he fucking comes is because he wants to have sex with you!"

The hurt and shock on Dana's face were palpable. Curt stood to his full height and grabbed Ryan's upper arm, his grip firm but not damaging. "That's no way to speak to your mother. Apologize and then sit down, so we can talk about this."

The boy ripped his arm from Curt's grasp. "Don't tell me what to do! You're not my father! I saw you kissing the other day when I came back to get my math book! How could you do that? I hate you!"

Before either of them could stop him, Ryan ran to the back door, yanked it open, and fled in a flurry of anger and resentment. Dana started after him, but Curt stopped her, gently cupping her cheek. "Let me handle this. Let me talk to him, man to boy-on-the-verge-of-becoming-a-man."

She bit her lip then nodded and wiped her tear-filled eyes. "Okay. I'll clean this up and start getting dinner ready."

After giving her a quick kiss, he headed to the backyard in search of Ryan, but found he was too late as he saw the boy disappear, riding his mountain bike on the trail leading into the woods. Deciding to let the kid cool off instead of chasing after him, Curt sat on the porch steps and stared at the mountain in the distance. "Eric, I could use a little help here. I love these kids like they were my own. I should have figured it would be hardest on Ryan, being the oldest and about to become a teenager. How do I convince him I'm not trying to replace you and I'll always make sure they remember you?"

Aside from the sounds of birds singing and the rustling of leaves, his question was met with silence. Dragging his hand down his face, he pondered what to say to the boy when he returned.

Ninety minutes later, though, Ryan hadn't returned and darkness was falling. The worry Dana felt was evident as she kept checking the clock on the microwave while she fed the other children at the kitchen table. He knew her thoughts were going back to the night Eric had gone missing and he couldn't wait any longer for Ryan to return. Standing behind Taylor, Curt squeezed the boy's shoulders. "Any idea where he would have gone?"

Taylor shrugged. "Probably the cave."

Curt's eyes narrowed as he glanced at Dana who didn't seem to know what her son was talking about. "What cave?"

"There's a cave we found while biking one day in the woods. Sometimes we go there to hunt for Indian arrowheads, but I don't know if we can find it in the dark. We've never tried."

Shit. He knew the boys had done a lot of exploring throughout the woods, but they never went there alone. Dana had always insisted they go in groups of three or more and stay with each other.

Justin piped up. "Mr. Olsen knows where it is. We showed it to him one day."

Grabbing his phone, Curt found Phil's number and pressed 'Send'. When the man answered, he told him, "I need you and your ATVs. Ryan and I had an argument and the boys think he went to some cave in the woods. That was over an hour and a half ago."

"Come on over. I'll pull the ATVs out of the barn and we'll go get him."

Hanging up the phone, Curt pulled Dana into an embrace and kissed her forehead when she briefly clung to him. "I'll have him back in no time. Don't worry."

Jogging a few houses down to the Olsen's, Curt found Phil all set to go with flashlights and his portable police radio, just in case. They mounted the ATVs and Phil took off into the woods with Curt on his tail. It took them a good ten minutes to reach the cave and with the moonlight hidden by some dark clouds, they had to rely on the ATVs' headlamps and the flashlights. Searching the area, they found no sign of Ryan or his bike. From the looks of things, the boy hadn't even been there as they couldn't find any fresh tire tracks or footprints.

The two men slowly rode back along the trail they hoped he had taken, looking for evidence of which way he might have gone. As they came around a large boulder, the light from Curt's headlamp flashed on something red about twenty feet off the trail and he hit the brakes. It was the reflector of a mountain bike. His heart pounding in his chest, he leaped over a downed tree and spotted Ryan lying among some shrubs and leaves. Dropping to his knees beside the boy, he was relieved to see him open his eyes even though they were filled with pain.

"Ry, what happened? Where are you hurt?"

"*Uhhhh*. My-my arm. A deer ran out in front of me and I lost control."

While Phil contacted his dispatcher to send an ambulance to the closest access point, Curt ran the beam of his flashlight over Ryan's arm and the rest of his body. Thankfully, despite his anger earlier, the kid had remembered to put on his helmet, which probably saved him from being hurt worse. As it was, it appeared his left forearm was broken.

92

Retrieving a blow-up splint from the first aid bag he'd brought along, Phil handed it to Curt, then very gently helped him apply it. Although he was in a lot of pain, Ryan did his best not to yell or cry. Once they had the limb immobilized, they gave him a once over to make sure there were no other injuries, then sat him up so they could carry him to Curt's ATV. Straddling the seat behind Ryan, Curt reached around and grasped the handles. Before he restarted the engine, Ryan turned his head so he could be heard. "I'm sorry, Uncle Curt. For everything. I didn't mean it."

Curt squeezed the boy's good arm so he was forgiven. "It's okay, sport. We'll talk about it later."

* * *

It was well after midnight when Dana and Curt returned home with Ryan from the emergency room. The arm had definitely been broken, but it was nothing a few weeks in a cast wouldn't heal. As Curt got the boy settled in his bed, Dana paid the college-aged woman who lived up the street and baby-sat for her often. Dana had called her as soon as Curt had gone back to the house to tell her what happened as Phil went in the ambulance with Ryan. He'd been torn between going with the boy or being the one to tell his mother he was en route to the hospital. But Ryan had made the decision easier, telling Curt it was okay for Phil to go with him while he went and got Dana.

After Ryan fell asleep from the painkillers he'd been given, Curt checked to make sure the other children were sleeping, then joined Dana in the master bedroom. Just wanting to hold her for a while, he mentally set his internal alarm clock and lay down beside her, pulling her into his side and wrapping his arms around her. At five a.m. he woke and reluctantly left her bed to go back to sleep on the couch so none of the kids would find them sleeping together until they had a chance to talk

93

with all of them.

Later that afternoon, Curt took the sandwich and glass of milk Dana had made for Ryan and brought them into the boy's bedroom. Handing him the plate, he placed the glass on the nightstand along with a pain pill for him to take when he was done eating. Ryan eyed him warily as Curt pulled over the room's desk chair and straddled it. "Think we can have a chat without yelling at each other?"

His question was met with a shoulder shrug and a mumbled, "I guess."

"Good." He inhaled deeply then let it out slowly. "I loved your dad, Ryan. More than you'll ever know. He was a brother to me and I would never, ever, try to replace him in your life...or your mom's life. But that doesn't mean I can't be here for all of you in a way he can't be. Your mom loved your dad with every bit of her heart and still does...and always will. But don't you want to see her happy again? What happens when you and your brothers and sister grow up and go out into the big world? Do you want your mom to be alone or with someone who loves her and will take care of her?" Ryan's eyes were focused on the sandwich on his lap which he made no effort to eat. "I don't come up here just for your mom. I'm here for the four of you, too. I made a promise to your dad a long time ago, that if anything ever happened to him, I would take care of all of you for him. I didn't expect to fall in love with your mom and vice versa—but we did." They had said those words to each other before falling asleep last night. "Your dad will always be the first love of her life...nothing will ever change that and I'm more than willing to accept it. But we need you to accept the fact that your mom and I love each other. And we love you, too. I hope you know you can come to me anytime you have a problem or even just to talk."

Deciding he'd said enough, Curt stopped talking and waited for Ryan to say something. The boy's eyes were still downcast. "Do we have to move to Daytona with you?"

He finally got it. The kid was worried about leaving behind not only his friends, but the place where he had the most memories of his father. "No, you don't. I haven't told your mom yet, since everything is so new between us, but I talked to my brother the other day. I told him I wanted to move up here and open another bike shop...sort of like a franchise."

Ryan's head whipped up, his eyes wide in surprise. "Really?"

Smiling, Curt nodded. "Yeah, really."

"Do you...will you teach me how to fix motorcycles?"

That was the last thing he expected to hear from him. "Seriously? You want to learn?"

"Yeah. My friend's older brother has one he's rebuilding. It's cool to watch him."

Hmmm. He'd have to find out if the brother was experienced and old enough to work in a shop. "Okay. Here's the deal. I'll teach you how to fix up bikes, and shave when you want, if you apologize to your mother...*and*...you agree to come to me like a grown-up if something I do or say bothers you. Deal?"

He held out his closed fist and Ryan bumped it with his own. "Deal."

"Okay. Now, since all of that is out of the way...I think it's time you and I had a little talk about the birds and the bees."

He grimaced when Ryan rolled his eyes...yeah, this talk was going to be a lot harder than the first one.

EPILOGUE

Two Years Later

"Open mine next, Papa Curtsy!"

He smiled as eight-year-old Amanda handed him a birthday present, which her mother had obviously helped her wrap. Winking at his wife of six months, he shook the small box and felt something heavy shift around inside. Outside at the picnic tables, he was surrounded by his mother, Eric's parents, the kids, and Dana, who now went by the hyphenated name Mrs. Prichard-Bannerman. It was something they had both agreed on so the children would never feel as if they'd pushed Eric from the family. They all had chosen different names for him. Ryan called him Pop. Taylor used Dad instead of Daddy, which is what he'd called Eric. And Justin told everyone Curt was his Pa.

"I wonder what this is?"

Amanda bounced on the balls of her feet in front of him. "Open it and find out!"

Everyone laughed at her exuberance as he tickled her side. "Good idea, short-stuff."

After tearing the paper off the square box, he held it up for everyone to see. "Someone remembered I wanted a new fishing reel."

"I did," the little girl announced with a look of pride and joy on her face.

"Well, thank you very much. And thanks to everyone for the gifts. It's been a great birthday." It really had been. In fact, it'd been a great year. His motorcycle shop had quickly gained the following it had in Florida and there was a waiting list for his design services. Dana was teaching again and loving every minute of it. They'd even finished Eric's dream of bringing some farm animals back to the property. They were now the proud owners of three pigs, two goats, ten chickens, and that same cocky rooster. They had also rescued two bullmastiffs from a rescue group Ian's friend Parker recommended, and the big lugs were sleeping in the shade of a nearby tree.

Fourteen-year-old Ryan stepped forward and handed him a shirt box which Curt hadn't noticed. "There's one more. This is from all of us."

Glancing up, Curt took it from him. He still couldn't get over how tall the kid had gotten in the past few months. He was probably going to end up being several inches over six feet.

As he started to open the present, he noticed Dana had begun filming him with her camera. "Just so you know, this was the kids' idea, and they had Grandpa help them with it. I just found out about it last week."

He squinted at Amanda and teased, "Short-stuff, how'd you keep a secret from me?"

Giggling, she shrugged as her brothers surrounded her. Taking the top of the box off, he moved aside the tissue paper and found...papers.

A stack of typed papers. Removing them, he read the top page and his eyes filled with tears. *Application for Adoption.*

Ryan pointed at the papers. "We want our last names to be Prichard-Bannerman, just like mom's.

Choked up, all he could do was open his arms and the children stepped forward to hug him in one big huddle. When he finally regained his composure, he looked each one in the eye before moving to the next. "You have no idea how much this means to me. I love you."

"We love you, too," they responded as one.

Standing, he shook hands with Earl, then kissed Alice and his own mother, all of whom were beaming at him. Lastly, he turned to his wife, who handed Ryan the still recording camera. She then took both of Curt's hands in hers and smiled at him. "There's one more present which no one else knows about. I'm pregnant."

Stunned, he just stared at her while all around him there were cheers and shouts of congratulations. Dropping to his knees in front of her, he placed his hand over her womb and his unborn child. "Hello, little Eric or Erica. I'm your daddy."

Towering over him, Dana gasped and he tilted his head so their gazes met. "What else would we call him or her?"

Happy tears ran down her cheeks as he got to his feet. Wrapping his arms around her, he shouted, "Family hug!" As the children joined them, Curt knew his best friend was watching over them, with his full approval, and always would be.

The End

ABOUT THE AUTHOR

Samantha A. Cole is a retired policewoman and former paramedic who has started a third career as an author. She has lived her entire life in the suburbs of New York City and has plans to become a 'snow-bird' between New York and Florida. Her two dogs, Jinx and Bella, keep her company and remind their 'mom' to take a break from writing every once in a while to go for a walk, of course with them in tow.

An avid reader since childhood, Samantha was often found with a book in hand and sometimes one in each. After being gifted with a stack of romance novels from her grandmother, her love affair with the genre began in her teens.

Samantha is continuing to work on the Trident Security series as well as a new trilogy, The Malone Brothers. She also has a few other stand-alone books in the works.

OTHER BOOKS BY SAMANTHA COLE

Leather & Lace: Trident Security Book 1 (Devon & Kristen)

His Angel: Trident Security Book 2 (Ian & Angie)

Waiting For Him: Trident Security Book 3 (Boomer & Kat)

Not Negotiable (Parker & Shelby)

Topping The Alpha: Trident Security Book 4 (Jake & Nick)

Watching From the Shadows: Trident Security Book 5 (Marco & Harper)

Coming Soon – Tickle His Fancy: Trident Security Book 6 (Brody & Fancy)

CONNECT WITH ME

Facebook: www.facebook.com/SamanthaColeAuthor

Amazon author page: http://www.amazon.com/Samantha-A.-Cole/e/B00X53K3X8

Website: https://samanthacoleauthor.wordpress.com

Twitter: https://twitter.com/SamanthaCole222

Google: https://plus.google.com/+SamanthaAColeAuthor

Goodreads: https://www.goodreads.com/author/show/5580362.Samantha_Cole

Instagram: https://www.instagram.com/samanthacoleauthor/

Pinterest: https://www.pinterest.com/samanthacoleaut/

51913765R00061

Made in the USA
Lexington, KY
09 May 2016